"You're Not Going To Marry Him," Alex Declared.

"But I—"

"But what? You love him? You expect me to believe that after the way you came apart in my arms?" He moved in on her, caging her between the desk and himself.

Desiree's pulse skittered at the fierce emotion emanating from him, at the desire burning hot and dark in those black eyes. Try as she might, she was unable to stop herself from responding to him. "Alex, you don't understand. If you'd just let me explain, Kevin and I—"

"I won't let you marry him."

And before she could say another word, he took possession of her mouth. Her mind. Her heart.

Dear Reader,

Where do you read Silhouette Desire? Sitting in your favorite chair? How about standing in line at the market or swinging in the sunporch hammock? Or do you hold out the entire day, waiting for all your distractions to dissolve around you, only to open a Desire novel once you're in a relaxing bath or resting against your softest pillow...? Wherever you indulge in Silhouette Desire, we know you do so with anticipation, and that's why we bring you the absolute best in romance fiction.

This month, look forward to talented Jennifer Greene's *A Baby in His In-Box,* where a sexy tutor gives March's MAN OF THE MONTH private lessons on sudden fatherhood. And in the second adorable tale of Elizabeth Bevarly's BLAME IT ON BOB series, *Beauty and the Brain,* a lady discovers she's still starry-eyed over her secret high school crush. Next, Susan Crosby takes readers on The Great Wife Search in *Bride Candidate #9.*

And don't miss a single kiss delivered by these delectable men: a roguish rancher in Amy J. Fetzer's *The Unlikely Bodyguard;* the strong, silent corporate hunk in the latest book in the RIGHT BRIDE, WRONG GROOM series, *Switched at the Altar,* by Metsy Hingle; and Eileen Wilks's mouthwatering honorable Texas hero in *Just a Little Bit Pregnant.*

So, no matter *where* you read, I know *what* you'll be reading— all six of March's irresistible Silhouette Desire love stories!

Regards,

Melissa Senate

Melissa Senate
Senior Editor
Silhouette Desire

Please address questions and book requests to:
Silhouette Reader Service
U.S.: 3010 Walden Ave., P.O. Box 1325, Buffalo, NY 14269
Canadian: P.O. Box 609, Fort Erie, Ont. L2A 5X3

METSY HINGLE
SWITCHED AT THE ALTAR

SILHOUETTE *Desire*®

Published by Silhouette Books

America's Publisher of Contemporary Romance

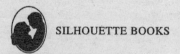

SILHOUETTE BOOKS

ISBN 0-373-76133-3

SWITCHED AT THE ALTAR

Copyright © 1998 by Metsy Hingle

Printed in U.S.A.

Books by Metsy Hingle

Silhouette Desire

Seduced #900
Surrender #978
Backfire #1026
Lovechild #1055
*The Kidnapped Bride #1103
*Switched at the Altar #1133

*Right Bride, Wrong Groom

METSY HINGLE

is a native of New Orleans, who loves the city in which she grew up. She credits the charm of her birthplace, and her own French heritage, with instilling in her the desire to write. Married and the mother of four children, she believes in romance and happy endings. Becoming a Silhouette author is a long-cherished dream come true for Metsy and one happy ending that she continues to celebrate with each new story she writes. She loves hearing from readers. Write to Metsy at P.O. Box 3224, Covington, LA 70433.

For the real "Maggie the Cat"
and her owner, Linda Kay West, a.k.a. Linda Lewis.

One

His brother was a dead man. Or at least he would be dead, Alexander Stone vowed, the moment he got his hands on him. Jerking open the door, he stepped inside Magnolia House. The lazy breeze of a ceiling fan stroked his skin like a woman's fingers as he moved into the entrance hall and out of the Louisiana heat.

Still cursing his younger sibling for causing him to make the trip from Boston to this backwater town outside of New Orleans, Alex marched over to the reception desk. He scowled at the sight of the unmanned desk before slapping the bell for assistance.

Temper curled like a fist in his gut as he waited and recounted the morning's discoveries. Not only had Kevin failed to show up for any of his summer law school classes for the past week, but he hadn't been seen at his apartment for even longer. Learning that his brother's mail was being forwarded to Magnolia House in care of

Ms. Desiree Mason had done nothing to improve his mood. Nor had it eased his rising temper. No wonder he hadn't been able to reach Kevin by phone for the past three days. The young fool had evidently moved in with the Mason woman.

The newspaper clipping—shoved under his nose by a former lady friend who'd come by to show off her engagement ring—flashed into Alex's mind's eye again.

What handsome younger son of one of Boston's finest families will soon be trading in his law books for a trip down the aisle with none other than a Southern belle of the stage…just as his dear, departed father did several times before him? Need a hint? The young man's older half-brother is a legal eagle and one of this city's most eligible bachelors. Still can't guess? How about this? The family name means hard, rocklike…as in a precious gem or *Stone*.

Even if he didn't have a genius IQ, Alex fumed, it wouldn't have been difficult for him to figure out that the scheming Ms. Desiree Mason had gotten her hooks firmly into his kid brother.

Well, he'd see how anxious the little gold digger was to marry Kevin once she found out that *he* was the one who controlled his trust fund.

Where the devil is everyone? Five seconds stretched into ten, obliterating what little patience he had left. Annoyed, Alex slapped the bell on the desk again.

Nothing. No one.

"Aw, the hell with it," he muttered. "I'll find Kevin myself." And when he did, he was through being a marshmallow where his younger brother was concerned. He'd been making that mistake from the day a nine-year-old Kevin had been deposited on his doorstep while their respective parents went off with their next set of spouses. In the thirteen years since then, he'd fought any and all objections to send Kevin away to military school, had even suffered their grandfather's anger for refusing to do so. But he'd been determined, hell-bent, on providing his brother with some semblance of a normal family, to give him a more nurturing childhood than the one he'd known.

And you've certainly done a fine job of it, Alex admonished himself silently. Look what a mess Kevin had gotten himself into now. And it was, at least partially, his fault. He should have known something like this would happen. Should have expected it. Kevin was a good-looking, wealthy young man—and far too easily swayed by a pretty face. Just as their father had been, Alex admitted. By giving in to Kevin's request to attend law school down south, he'd all but thrown Kevin to the wolves. And he'd allowed his brother to become the target of every sweet, magnolia vamp south of the Mason-Dixon line trying to land herself a rich husband.

And evidently Ms. Desiree Mason had scored a bull's-eye.

Alex gritted his teeth. The woman's name alone should have set off alarm bells the first time Kevin had mentioned her. His kid brother was no match for some conniving, Southern belle with a honey-voiced accent. Well, Ms. Desiree Mason would have to find herself some other young fool to marry, because he had no intention of letting his brother make the biggest mistake of his life.

As of right now, Kevin was going to be made to toe the line. And he was going to start by going back to law school—in Boston, not New Orleans—and forgetting any foolish thoughts he might have about marrying Desiree Mason. With that idea in mind, Alex started down the hall in search of his brother. He froze mid-stride at the sound of an all-too-familiar tune. It was the one song that he had sworn both of his parents had adopted as their personal favorite, the one song that still made him break out in a cold sweat whenever he heard it.

The wedding march!

Panic sent adrenaline rushing through his body, and Alex sped down the length of the hall toward the sound of the music. The last cords of the tune faded just as he jerked open the massive double doors to a ballroom.

"Dearly beloved..."

Alex bit back an oath at the sight of bridesmaids, groomsmen, a minister holding a bible. His gaze darted to the back of the shapely redhead in the wedding dress and stared at bare shoulders, the color of rich cream, that flirted beneath a whisper of lace. Swallowing hard, Alex dragged his gaze from the bride to the groom standing beside her. His heart stopped and then started again as he looked at the familiar back of the tall, dark-haired man about to be married—his brother, Kevin.

"We are gathered here today to join this man and this woman in the sacrament of holy matrimony," the minister continued. "Marriage is a—"

"Stop," Alex shouted. Heedless of the surprised gasps and curious looks directed at him, he raced down the aisle. "I demand you stop this wedding at once!"

The bride whipped around. Her blue-green eyes widened with shock. Twin spots of color climbed her cheeks. Alex stared at those rose-colored lips rounded in surprise. Crazily, for the space of a heartbeat, he wondered what it would be like to sample that mouth.

"How dare you?" she demanded.

"Quite easily," Alex shot back, shaking off his strange reaction to the woman. He curled his hands into fists at his sides as he realized that in another two minutes he would have been too late. "There's no way I'm going to allow you to marry my brother."

Dismissing the round of gasps that went up and the furious look the bride cast his way, Alex shifted his attention to his brother. He waited, braced for Kevin's outburst.

"Oh, that was perfect!"

Alex yanked his attention back to the bride at the same time that she launched herself at him. Not stopping to think, he caught her in his arms, holding on to her at the waist. But instead of hitting him as he expected, she proceeded to curl her arms around his neck.

He snagged her wrists, sure she was intent on strangling him. "Listen, lady—"

She cut off his protest with her mouth. Alex sucked in a breath at the feel of those soft lips brushing against his own. Desire—unexpected and unwanted—put fire in his belly, raced to his loins.

Suddenly she was pulling her mouth free and staring at him. Judging by her stunned expression and the confusion in those blue-green eyes of hers, he wasn't the only one who'd felt as though he'd just been whacked by a thunderbolt. It was insane, Alex told himself. But he couldn't stop himself from sliding his gaze to that ripe, lush mouth of hers again. Desire, sweet and aching, bit at him once more.

As though sensing his thoughts, she tugged her wrists free and eased back one step, then another. She gave him a lazy smile and followed with a single "Wow!"

"Wow" was right, Alex thought. Still reeling from the unexpected kiss and its effect on him, he shook his head to clear the sensuous fog that seemed to have ensnared him.

"Hey, that was pretty good," one of the bridesmaids called out.

Good? Good didn't even come close to describing that kiss or the strange way it had made him feel. And since when does a bridesmaid critique a kiss delivered to the intended bride by a stranger?

The bride spun around, presenting him with another view of her back and more cream-colored skin where her dress dipped along her shoulders. She headed toward the critiquing bridesmaid. "Didn't I tell you guys that Bernie would come through for us?" she exclaimed in a voice that was decidedly huskier than it had been a few moments ago.

A voice that reminded him of sultry summer nights and hot sex, Alex decided. He sucked in a breath. What in the hell was wrong with him? Lusting after the little gold digger who'd been about to marry his brother.

His brother! Alex nearly groaned. Oh, Lord, he'd forgotten about Kevin. He jerked his attention back to his brother. But instead of getting ready to charge over and tear into him for interfering, Kevin had one arm draped around his kissing bride and the other one around a bridesmaid and was chatting with them as though nothing had happened. Frowning, Alex started toward him. "Kev—"

The minister blocked his path. "You cut in too soon," the reverend admonished, pointing an accusing finger in his face. "Why didn't you wait for me to give you your cue?"

Alex frowned at the portly clergyman. His cue?

"Yeah. You were supposed to wait for your cue," the best man informed him.

"Hey, they're right, pal," the groom added as he came

over to join them. "You cut in before I got a chance to deliver my lines."

Alex sucked in his breath as he stared at the face of the groom. The guy was dark-haired, brown-eyed and just about Kevin's height and size. He even had an endearing choirboy grin that was similar to his brother's.

Only he *wasn't* his brother.

Relief rushed through Alex like water overflowing a swollen creek. Kevin *hadn't* been on the verge of marrying the sexy redhead after all. But on the heels of that revelation came an equally disturbing and surprisingly disappointing one. The woman he'd been lusting after for the past sixty seconds *was* about to marry someone.

And he'd just interrupted her wedding.

"Are you OK?" the bride asked him as she came back to stand before him. "You look…upset."

"No. It's just that I thought… That is, I didn't realize…" Alex clamped his mouth firmly shut, chagrined to be stumbling over his words like a tongue-tied teenager in the throes of his first crush. After a moment, he tried again. "I'm terribly sorry."

"Whatever for?" she asked in that soft, honeyed voice. "You were great."

He was great? "I'm afraid I—"

She smiled at him again, and Alex forgot what he'd been about to say. Cursing himself, he took a deep breath. He had to get out of here. "I'm sorry. I can see now that I made a mistake. Please accept my apologies for the, um, interruption. I'll just leave you and your…your…"

He flicked a glance at the groom he'd mistaken for his brother. The man appeared to be making time with the bridesmaid. Alex swallowed. "I'll just get out of your way and let you get back to your wedding." Without wasting another moment, he turned to leave.

"Wait!" She caught his arm before he'd managed to take the first step. "Listen, I know I said you were great, and you were, but I still think it could use some work. Why don't we try it again? Just do everything exactly the same way you did a few minutes ago."

Alex's jaw dropped. His body tensed. He couldn't help it. His gaze fell to her lips and he felt that slap of heat again. "You want me to kiss you again?"

"Well, yes. That, too." She gave him another of those lazy smiles that did strange things to his brain and made it difficult for him to think clearly. "But this time, be sure to wait for your cue."

Alex blinked. "My cue?"

"Yes. When the reverend asks if there are any objections, that's where you're supposed to come in. Otherwise, do everything exactly the way you did it a minute ago," she instructed him. "Your inflection was perfect, and I loved the ad lib, by the way. It was a nice touch. You can go ahead and leave it in."

His inflection? The ad lib? What in the hell was she talking about?

"Oh, and be sure to do that steely-eyed thing that you did with your eyes again. For a minute there, you even had *me* believing you were serious about stopping the wedding."

"I *was* serious," Alex countered, growing more confused by the second. "I thought—" His tongue twisted in his mouth as she curved her lips into another one of those smiles and sent fire singing through his veins. "Damn!"

Her smile slipped. "What is it? What's wrong?"

Alex took a long, measured breath and struggled to regain control of the situation and of himself. "Lady, I don't have a clue as to what you're talking about."

She tipped her head and eyed him curiously. "What is it you don't understand?"

"I don't understand anything you've said. I don't know a thing about any cues or ad libs or steely-eyed looks. If I was convincing when I came in here and demanded you stop the wedding it's because I thought I *was* stopping a wedding."

"You thought this was a *real* wedding?"

"Yes."

She narrowed her eyes. "And just whose wedding did you think you were stopping?"

"My brother's." He squeezed his eyes shut a moment, mortified to have made such a mistake. For a smart man who was considered to be great when it came to assessing businesses, he had just scored a big, fat zero in assessing this situation. If he'd been the least bit astute, he would have noted earlier what he saw now—a stage at the far end of the room, drapes drawn across that stage and a sign tacked to one curtain that read Wet Paint.

"I see," she said, sighing. "Then I guess Bernie didn't send you after all."

Exasperated, Alex dragged a hand through his hair. "I don't even know anyone named Bernie."

"I was afraid of that. I don't suppose there's any chance that you're an unemployed actor looking for work, is there?" she asked hopefully.

Alex almost laughed at the notion, and he would have if he weren't feeling as though he'd wandered into the Twilight Zone. "Hardly. I'm an attorney. My name's Alex Stone."

Desiree nearly choked. This was Alexander Stone? This giant of a man with the eyes of a warrior and the face of a dark angel? This man whose kiss had made her blood spin? *He* was Kevin's uptight, stuffy, older brother?

Desiree caught her bottom lip between her teeth as she studied him more closely. Of course, she could see his resemblance to Kevin now. And if she hadn't been so wrapped up in the play and her reaction to him, maybe she *would* have spotted the similarities sooner. After all, the two men did share those same dark, good looks. But where Kevin's hair curled a bit and brushed his collar, Alex's was stick straight and shorter, making that sharp jaw of his appear even sharper—and for some reason more appealing to her. And where Kevin's eyes were a warm brown that had roused an immediate sisterly affection in her, Alex's eyes were hard and as black as a moonless sky. And when he'd looked at her, when those midnight eyes of his had snapped to life with desire, she had in no way been inclined with feelings that were sisterly.

Nope, Alexander Stone didn't make her feel the least bit sisterly, Desiree admitted as she continued to study him. In fact, she couldn't help wondering what it would be like to *really* be kissed by him.

Like jumping from the frying pan into the fire, she told herself. Not only would it be stupid, but she didn't have the time or the inclination to let her hormones get in the way. At least not now. Not when she had a dinner theater set to open in less than a month, and not when one of her players was still missing.

"And you are…?"

Desiree dragged her attention to Alex's outstretched hand. As she placed her fingers in his palm, a shiver of awareness shimmied down her spine. Well, what do you know, she thought, a bit excited by her reaction to him. Ever since her sister Lorelei's kidnapping and wedding a few months before to the man who'd been her first love, she'd found herself daydreaming and wishing she would meet someone special. And now here was Alexander Stone. "Desiree. My name's Desiree."

Alex's fingers tightened around hers. "Desiree? *You're* Desiree Mason?"

"Yes," she said, surprised that he knew her full name, as well as by his quick release of her hand. "Did Kevin happen to mention me to you?"

"Oh, yes. He's mentioned you all right."

And judging by Alex's chilled tone and the way his jaw had clenched, whatever Kevin had told his big brother about her hadn't been to Alex's liking.

"You're the actress."

He made the term *actress* sound as though it ranked right up there with the word *thief*. "Yes, I am."

"I see," he said coolly.

Talk about rotten karma. "It figures," Desiree muttered. It was just her luck that the first man she'd been attracted to in ages would be a stick-in-the-mud Adonis in a custom-tailored suit with a chip the size of a boulder on his linebacker shoulders.

"What figures?"

"That you were just too good to be true."

"I beg your pardon?"

Desiree doubted that Alexander Stone ever had to beg for anything—especially not from a woman. She shrugged. No way would she admit her foolish romantic thoughts to him or anyone else. "I was just thinking you're a good actor," she replied instead. "Too good for me to have mistaken you for a green drama student."

"Thank you. I think."

"If you ever decide to change professions, you should keep acting in mind. You'd be great on the stage."

"I don't think there's much chance of that happening."

Desiree grinned at his clipped reply. He looked as though even the thought of doing such a thing would be about as pleasant as a toothache. "One never knows. There are an awful lot of lawyers out there."

"And according to statistics, there are just about as many would-be actors."

"Probably because there are so many out-of-work lawyers. But I guess it's to be expected."

"And how do you figure that?"

"Well, from what I've seen of the legal system, there's not a lot of difference between acting and lawyering. One uses a stage and the other uses a courtroom."

"So what gives, Des?" Charlie, the play's minister, called out. "We gonna rehearse anymore or not?"

"Not," she told him. Lifting the train of her wedding dress, she brushed past Alex and stepped to the center of the room. She clapped her hands. "All right, everybody. Listen up. That's it for today. But I want everyone here tomorrow morning at eight o'clock sharp."

"Eight o'clock?"

"That's right. Eight o'clock," Desiree said, ignoring the groans. "And I don't want anyone to be late."

"What about breakfast?" O'Reilly, her groom, asked.

Desiree grinned. The only thing that O'Reilly loved more than the ladies was food. "I'll see what Harry can scrape up for you guys. Just make sure you're here on time."

The old ballroom hummed with the sound of voices and shuffling feet as the cast began to file out. Try as she might to ignore him, Desiree was all too conscious of Alex standing right where she'd left him. She could feel his gaze fastened on her as she saw the others out, studying her relentlessly as though she were some strange new species of bug under a microscope.

She cut a glance to him and watched those dark eyes of his slide over her, then ease back up to linger on her mouth. Her traitorous pulse jumped as she remembered their kiss. Suddenly it was there again. That breath-stealing awareness between them. Quickly she turned away and drew in a steadying breath. She must have taken leave of her senses. No way did she want to get involved with Alex Stone. The two of them would be like oil and water. For starters, from everything Kevin had told her, his brother liked the females and they liked him, but the man was definitely antimarriage. While she...she wanted to get married someday and find the "happily ever after" her parents and her sister had discovered. She started toward the mock church railing to retrieve the silk bridal bouquet she'd left there.

With a speed that surprised her, Alex was moving in front of her, blocking her path. "Aren't you the least bit interested as to why I'm here, Ms. Mason? Or why I thought you were marrying my brother?"

At five feet eight inches Desiree didn't have to look up to find herself on eye level with most men—especially not when she was wearing three-inch heels as she was now. But with Alex, she found herself tipping her head back. "I assumed you were looking for Kevin."

"That's right."

"And as you can see, he isn't here. But don't worry, I'll be sure to let him know you came by." Reaching past him, she scooped up the bouquet with one hand, then picked up the skirts of her wedding gown with the other. "Now if you'll excuse me, I have to go change."

Alex caught her arm before she could take a step. "Not

so fast, Ms. Mason. I do believe you and I need to have a little chat.''

Desiree blew at the wisp of hair that drifted across one eye. "I don't think there's anything for us to discuss. That is, not unless you're interested in auditioning for the play."

"Afraid I'll have to pass."

She shrugged. "Your decision. And since I don't have the time or the inclination to discuss the merits of acting with you, I'd appreciate it if you'd let go of my arm." She looked down at the large hand circling her forearm and back up at him. "That is, unless you'd like to have me demonstrate some of the new moves I've learned in my karate class."

Alex released her, but continued to block her path.

Exasperated, she said, "Mr. Stone, I'm a busy woman. And I've got a dinner theater to run. I strongly suggest you get out of my way." Before she gave in to the impulse to kick him in the shins, she added silently.

"And I'm a busy man with a law firm and a major corporation back in Boston to run, but I—"

"Then I'd suggest you start for the airport," she said. "You've got about an hour's drive ahead of you."

"As I started to say, I'm not leaving here until we have a little discussion about you and my brother and I get some answers."

"Answers to what?"

"To questions like whose idea was it for Kevin to drop out of law school?"

Desiree hesitated, chewing on that bit of news. "I wasn't aware that Kevin had dropped out." In fact, Kevin hadn't said a word about doing any such thing when he'd told her he was going to Chicago to visit his sweetheart and audition for a new show. He'd only asked if he could have his mail forwarded to her while he was gone.

"Weren't you?"

She didn't miss the accusation in his tone. "No, I wasn't." But thanks to Kevin, she *was* all too aware of Alex's displeasure at his brother's interest in theater. It was the excuse Kevin had given her for not telling Alex the truth—that he wanted to be an actor, not an attorney. As the youngest of three girls, she knew all about putting up with older siblings who thought they knew what was best for you and ended up trying to run your life. "But if Kevin has decided to leave law school, I'd say that's his decision and not yours."

"Or yours?" Alex countered.

"No," she returned, frowning. "Why on earth would you think it was my decision?"

"Why indeed. Come off it, Ms. Mason," he said, his voice as sharp as the look he gave her. "Kevin told me when he was home during the holidays what close friends the two of you had become. I just hadn't realized how close that relationship was. I'm sure your opinion on the subject of his attending law school would have had a great deal to do with his decision."

Desiree pursed her lips. Evidently dear Kevin had also failed to explain the nature of their friendship to his brother. Given Alex's reaction, she could understand why. She glanced up, read the disapproval and suspicion in his eyes. Temper spiked through her again. The heck with setting him straight. The man deserved to stew a bit, and she intended to make him do just that. "Well, you're right about one thing. Kevin and I have become *very* close friends," she said in her best imitation of a vamp's voice.

Alex's dark eyes grew stormy, and Desiree told herself

she'd been right in her initial assessment of him. The man did have the eyes of a warrior—hard, cold, uncompromising. "But as far as law school goes, you give me far too much credit. The only opinion that really matters is Kevin's. After all, the decision is his to make. Not yours or mine."

The smile he gave her sent a ripple of uneasiness down Desiree's spine. "True. But what does matter is that *I'm* the one who controls Kevin's trust fund."

"Bully for you," she quipped, feigning indifference. Trust fund? What trust fund? She'd assumed Kevin's family had a bit of money. Anyone with brains in their head could see that he dressed well, drove a nice car, and while he wasn't flashy with money, he never seemed to be short of it. Besides, he was attending a prestigious and pricy law school in New Orleans. That in itself would have wiped out any scenarios about him being on the verge of poverty. Still, the way Alex had spit out the words *trust fund,* she doubted he was talking about a few thousand dollars—which had been the most her savings book had ever managed to reflect. "I still don't see how that affects me."

"Don't you?"

"No. I'd say that's between you and Kevin. After all, it's Kevin's life."

"Yes, it is," Alex said in a deadly soft voice. "And I have no intention of standing by and letting Kevin ruin his life by marrying you."

Shock hit her first, then her anger kicked into high gear. She strangled the stem of the bouquet in her hand and silently condemned Kevin to a slow, painful death for getting her into this fix in the first place. Tipping up her chin up, she called on her training as an actress to make her lips curve into a smile that reached her eyes.

She batted her lashes in what she hoped reflected all sweetness and innocence. ''Well then,'' she said laying on the Southern drawl like thick maple syrup. ''I guess I'll just have to be sure to tell Kevin not to bother sending you an invitation to the wedding.''

Two

For a moment Alex couldn't speak. He nearly choked
on the fury rising inside him. "There isn't going to be a
wedding," he finally managed to say.

Desiree arched her brow. "No? I wouldn't be so sure
of that."

"I *am* sure of it. Kevin is *not* going to marry you."

"I believe that's another one of those decisions that's
not yours to make."

"Trust me, Ms. Mason. You are not going to marry
my brother." Even if he was wrong and she wasn't a
gold-digging actress with her eye on Kevin's trust fund
as he suspected, he couldn't tolerate the thought of her
being married to his brother. Not when he could all too
easily imagine her with him, in *his* bed, with her body
naked beneath his. Just the thought of being with her had
him growing hard with desire—and sent guilt stabbing
through him like a knife. He shoved a hand through his

hair. She was involved with his brother, for pity's sake. Yet, not even that knowledge could ease the hungry, restless ache inside him that he experienced by just looking at her.

"Like I said, that's Kevin's decision. And mine," she amended a moment later, as though adding herself to the equation was an afterthought. "Now, you really will have to excuse me while I see if I can find out what happened to the actor Bernie was supposed to send over."

She smiled at him, and Alex's brain turned to mush. He stared at her mouth, mesmerized by the bow shape of those rose-colored lips, remembering how warm and soft they'd felt against his own.

"I believe you can find your way out."

He watched in silence as she scooped up the train of her wedding gown and walked down the hall. For a second he tracked the enticing sway of her hips as she moved down the corridor before she disappeared into one of the rooms.

At the click of the door closing, Alex blinked. He shook his head to clear it. Muttering an oath, he started off after her. "The woman must be some kind of witch," Alex grumbled, remembering the tales of voodoo and black magic that was supposedly still practiced in the New Orleans area. For a moment he'd been so mesmerized by her that he'd almost forgotten his reason for being here in the first place. Alex frowned at that realization. Try as he might to stop it, he couldn't help thinking of his father.

Eddie Stone had been a dashing, debonair ladies' man with a hearty laugh, a lust for partying and the deep pockets to pay for it. He'd also been as irresponsible as hell. He'd been about to marry wife number five when he'd been killed in a skiing accident. Otherwise, Alex might have added a few more stepmothers to his family tree. While his memories of time spent with his father were good ones, they were far too few—primarily because of his string of ex-wives, three of whom had been ladies from the South.

And now Kevin thought he was in love with Desiree Mason, another Southern belle. He conjured up an image of the green-eyed beauty in his mind and frowned. Maybe it was something in the water that drew men to women like her. Alex hesitated in front of the room he'd seen Desiree go into. Or maybe it was a weak gene in the Stone men that made them susceptible to a woman with a honeyed voice and magnolia-soft skin.

Whatever the reason, Alex decided, *he* had no intention of allowing himself to fall under Desiree Mason's or any woman's spell. With that thought in mind, he rapped his knuckles on the door.

"It's open," she called out in a distant, somewhat muffled voice.

Alex pushed the door open and stepped inside only to discover the room was empty. "Ms. Mason?"

"Be right with you," Desiree called out from an adjoining room.

As he waited, Alex took the opportunity to study the room. Just like the rest of the house, this room boasted high ceilings that were accented by crown molding. Ivory silk wall coverings flecked with gold ran from ceiling to floor. What he suspected was either a genuine Aubusson rug or a good imitation covered the center of a wooden floor that was in dire need of polishing. A lovely watercolor of Magnolia House and the grounds, painted during earlier and obviously more prosperous times, hung crookedly on one wall alongside several framed theater posters of plays that he'd never heard of, let alone seen.

On another wall damask drapes, in a faded shade of what once had probably been mint, were swept back from a massive window that served as a home to a half dozen flowering plants.

Alex fingered a purple bloom on one of the plants and caught the fragrant scent. Wisteria. It brought back vague memories of a house with a yard and a huge tree with a swing. He could remember sitting in that swing as a little boy, urging his mother to push him higher. He'd wanted to reach the tree's limbs and capture one of the purple flowers from the vine tangled in its branches. It had been the first and only time he'd lived with his parents—before they'd divorced, before they'd left him with his grandfather and gone on to their new lives—lives without him.

Pushing the melancholy thought aside, Alex prowled the room while he waited for Desiree. The place was a mess, Alex decided as he looked at the beautiful Queen Anne desk covered with stacks of papers, magazines and bound copies of what were evidently plays. A battered-looking computer sat haphazardly on a desk blotter. Framed photographs took up what little space was left. Alex picked up one of the snapshots of a much-younger Desiree flanked by a timid-looking blonde and a serious-eyed brunette—all dressed in toy soldier costumes and tap shoes. He grinned at the way Desiree mugged for the camera despite two missing front teeth.

"That was one of my first starring roles," Desiree told him from the doorway. "You're looking at the Mason Sisters Trio. Tap dance recital for four- to six-year-olds," she explained.

She was still wearing the wedding dress, but the veil and flowers were gone. Most of her hair had escaped from its combs, leaving long strands of red shot with gold trailing along her neck and cheeks. "Must have been quite a performance," Alex replied.

"Oh, believe me, it was."

She walked toward him, the sound of her skirt swishing as she moved, and his eyes immediately zeroed in on those sashaying hips.

"My sister Lorelei—she's the blonde—lost her dinner in front of the entire audience before we even got to the first 'ball-change' in the dance routine. Stage fright," she said as though that explained everything.

"And my sister Clea—" she pointed to the brunette "—she's the perfectionist. She was so miffed at Lorelei for ruining our act, she walked off the stage in the middle of our number and hung up her tap shoes for good. I'm afraid it ruined any hopes my parents might have been harboring that we'd be a dancing version of the Lennon Sisters."

"What about you? What did you do when your sisters dropped out of the show?"

"The Mason Sisters Trio quickly became a group of one. They had to yank me off the stage because I insisted on completing the number by doing everyone's part."

Alex heard the smile in her voice even before she looked up from the photograph he was holding and he saw it on her lips. "And you've been dancing ever since."

"And acting." She took the picture from his hands, stroked the edges of the frame lovingly before returning it to her desk. She glanced up at him. "But I'm sure you didn't really follow me in here to hear about my sisters and our failed attempt at show business, now, did you?"

"No." He hadn't, and Alex tamped down the urge to ask her to tell him more about herself and her family. Once more the lady had distracted him from his purpose.

"I'm here because we didn't finish our conversation about you and Kevin."

"We did as far as I'm concerned. There's nothing further to discuss." Desiree turned around, offering him her back. "Do me a favor, will you? Unhook the back of this thing so I can get out of this dress."

Alex stared at her bare shoulders and tried to ignore the faint hint of flowers that seemed to emanate from her skin. His gaze strayed to a heart-shaped mole just above her left shoulder. He had an incredible urge to run his fingertip across it.

"I had Mindy—she was one of the bridesmaids—help me get into this getup, but she's already gone, and now I can't get the thing off by myself. I can't imagine why a designer would make a dress with all those tiny buttons down the back. How do they expect you to get the thing off?"

"Since it's a wedding dress, I suspect the designer assumed the bride's husband would be helping her to take it off."

Desiree stilled a moment, and then he heard her laughter. "Kevin said you tended to take things literally. He was right." She looked at him over her shoulder again. Her green eyes sparkled, a mischievous grin curved her mouth. "Well, since my groom isn't here at the moment, maybe you could do the honors for him. Or is that a problem?"

Alex caught the note of challenge in her voice, saw the dare in her eyes. "No problem at all." He'd show the little tease. Did she think she could unnerve him by asking him to help her undress? He reached for the first button. His fingers brushed against her skin, and it was just as soft as it looked. And warm. Despite his efforts not to respond to her and all that soft, bare skin, the blood heated in his veins as, one by one, he released the tiny buttons from their silken loops. "There. It's unbuttoned," he told her and stepped back.

Clutching the front of her gown with one hand, she reached behind her to the bow at her waist. She fumbled with the fastening. She turned slightly and lifted her gaze to his. The challenge was still there in her eyes, but there was also an awareness now that hadn't been there a moment ago. "Looks like I need you to unhook the train for me, too," she told him in that honey and whiskey voice before giving him her back again. "There's a row of hooks beneath the bow."

Alex felt the punch of desire hit him as he forced his gaze down the length of her bare spine where the dress gaped, to the curve of her waist, to the jutting of her hips.

"Can you see the hooks?"

"I see them," he said, irritated by his body's response to her. Swallowing, Alex hesitated a moment before stepping closer. He lifted the bow that draped over her shapely bottom and, gritting his teeth, he fought back the urge to cup her in his hands. Instead, he caught her at the waist with his right hand and used the fingers of his left hand to work at the tiny hooks attached to the bow. All the while he was conscious of the slope of her hips, the warmth of the satin-covered skin beneath his fingers.

Finally the bow and train fell free from the gown. After placing them on the desk, he started to attack the row of buttons that ran from her waist to the top of her bottom. He'd barely finished opening the first button when Desiree reached behind her and grabbed his hand.

"Stop!"

Alex looked up, surprised at the unsteady sound of her voice. She whipped around. Still holding the front of her dress, she snatched up the train and bow with one hand

and took a few steps away from him. When she looked at him, heat licked at him again as he recognized the flame of desire in her eyes. He slid his gaze down the length of her and back up again, noting her flushed cheeks, her quickened breathing, the rise and fall of her breasts. Alex itched to reach out, pull her fingers away from where they clutched the front of the dress to her. He wanted to peel the lace edges away from her breasts and touch them. He took a step toward her.

Desiree moved a step back. "Th-thanks. But I think I can manage the rest of the buttons myself," she told him, then began to inch her way backward across the room until she reached the door she'd emerged from earlier. She fumbled with the doorknob, pushed the door open with the heel of her foot. "Goodbye, Alex. I'll tell Kevin you were looking for him," she said before disappearing behind the door.

Alex took a deep breath. He scrubbed a hand across his face. Muttering an oath, he jammed his hands into his pockets. No wonder Kevin was in trouble! Hell, *he* had been in trouble there for a minute. The woman had him feeling like a damn teenager who'd just discovered the opposite sex. Another five minutes of touching her soft flesh, smelling that flower-scented skin and *he* would have been hard-pressed not to beg her to let him make love to her.

Kevin was definitely in over his head where Desiree Mason was concerned. His brother wouldn't have a prayer at resisting the woman if she'd set her sights on marrying him. His only hope, Alex decided, was to find Kevin fast and get his brother back to Boston and as far away from Desiree Mason as he possibly could. It also wouldn't be a bad idea to get himself out of range as well.

Desiree leaned against the door of her bedroom. Closing her eyes, she took a deep breath. Whew! Talk about playing with fire. Alexander Stone ranked right up there with a four-alarm blaze. She must have been out of her mind to bait him the way she had. Pushing away from the door, she finished unbuttoning the wedding dress and shivered as she remembered the feel of his fingers brushing against her skin. Her stomach fluttered as she recalled glancing up and seeing the heat of desire in his dark eyes.

Thank heavens she'd had enough sense to call a halt to things when she had. Otherwise, who knows what would have happened. Desiree frowned. From everything Kevin had told her about his older brother and his aversion to romantic involvements, she didn't doubt for a moment that she'd have been the one who would have ended up getting burned.

She arranged the gown on its padded hanger and did up some of the buttons to keep it in place. As she fingered the satin-covered buttons, she thought of Alex's comment about the dress being designed for a man to take it off. A tremor of excitement danced along her spine as she wondered what it would have been like to have Alex undress her for real.

Dangerous, she told herself at the crazy thought. *Give it up, girl. The man is definitely not the "marriage and happily ever after" type.* And since she wasn't interested in an affair, there was no point in even thinking about it. She reached for a pair of white cotton shorts and the tropical-print blouse that she'd laid out on the bed earlier. She should be thanking her lucky stars she'd gotten rid of the man, she chided. But instead of relief, she felt an odd sense of disappointment.

Desiree laughed aloud at herself. Evidently catching the bouquet at her sister Lorelei's wedding and then taking on the role of a bride in this play had fried her brain. Why else would she be the least bit disappointed to see the last of Alexander Stone? The guy might be gorgeous and maybe he could make her blood spin with just a look, but she'd have to be nuts to even consider getting involved with him. Not that there was much likelihood of that happening, since he believed she was engaged to his brother.

She felt a prick of conscience at that thought. She probably shouldn't have let him think that she and Kevin were engaged. But even if she'd come clean and told him the truth—that she and Kevin were nothing more than friends—he probably wouldn't have believed her, anyway. He'd made up his mind, before he'd known who she was, that she was after Kevin for his money. Well, Alex Stone would have to just stew over her pretend engagement to his brother until Kevin returned, and then he could set the man straight. In the meantime she was short one actor and had yet to speak to Bernie.

After knotting the blouse at her waist, she slipped on her sandals and headed out the door. She stepped into the sitting room that she'd converted into her office and headed straight for her desk to find Bernie's number. She came to a halt mid-step at the sight of Alex standing at the window, staring out at the oak trees. Her chest tightened at the sad, lonely expression on his face.

As though sensing her presence he turned around to face her. The vulnerability that had been there a moment ago disappeared. His eyes darkened. He slid his gaze over her like a caress, and Desiree's disobedient pulse immediately picked up speed. With far more calm than she was feeling, she walked over to her desk. Retrieving the stack of business cards she'd bundled together with a rubber band weeks ago and had yet to organize, she began to shuffle through them in search of Bernie's phone number. "I didn't realize you were still here," she told him, praying he wouldn't notice how unsteady her fingers were.

"Contrary to what you might prefer, I have no intention of leaving until I speak with my brother."

"But I told you, Kevin isn't here."

"I know what you said. But I don't believe you. I wouldn't put it past Kevin to hide out just to avoid facing me. He knew I'd be furious with him for dropping out of law school, and he knows I'd be even angrier at the prospect of him getting married."

"Fine, don't believe me then," she said, slapping down the cards. Lord, but the man was stubborn. "Since you're so convinced I'm lying, why don't you search the house and grounds."

"I intend to."

She shrugged. "Suit yourself. It's your time. If you want to waste it, go right ahead. But you aren't going to find Kevin hidden under a bed or a closet somewhere because I told you the truth. Your brother *isn't* here."

Alex rubbed his jaw and continued to study her with those midnight eyes of his. "If he's not here, then where is he?"

"Out of town."

"Out of town?"

"That's what I said. He left more than a week ago."

"Where did he go?"

"I...I don't know," Desiree replied and crossed her fingers behind her back at the semi-white lie. Well, it was true, she reasoned. She *didn't* know exactly where Kevin was, only that he was somewhere in the Chicago area. He'd gone to visit his girlfriend—a dancer working in a musical.

"When is he due back?"

"I'm not exactly sure."

Alex narrowed his eyes. "You expect me to believe that my brother drops out of law school, closes up his apartment and leaves town without telling his fiancée where he's going or when he'll be back?"

"Yes! No!"

"Well, which one is it?" Alex demanded.

"Both." She took a steadying breath and wished she'd never let herself get into this mess. "Listen, I'm telling you the truth. I don't know where Kevin is or when he'll be back because...well, because I sort of misled you a little earlier," she admitted, embarrassed now by how she'd let her temper get the better of her.

"Misled me?"

Desiree could feel the flush crawl up her neck and cheeks. "About...about the nature of my relationship with Kevin," she finally managed to get out. Feeling defensive, she tried to explain. "You were acting so darn huffy when you came in here looking like you'd just stepped out of an advertisement in *GQ* with your custom-made suit and Italian loafers and you were so darned indignant at the mere idea that Kevin might actually consider marrying me that I...that I—" she hiked up her chin "—I decided to teach you a lesson."

"A lesson," he repeated.

"Yes, about that snooty attitude of yours."

"Snooty?"

"Yes, snooty."

Alex's frown deepened. "Go on. We'll debate your assessment of my attitude another time. Right now why don't you explain just how you misled me."

"I let you think that Kevin and I are engaged, when we're not. The truth is, he and I are just good friends."

Alex clapped his hands in mock approval. "Very good, Ms. Mason. That was a nice little performance and delivered with such sincerity. The wringing of your hands and halted speech was especially convincing. I can see why you chose acting as a profession. You're quite good at it. Unfortunately for you, I happen to know you're lying through your pretty, white teeth."

"What?" Desiree shrieked, shocked that despite her confession the man still didn't believe her.

"You heard me. I don't believe a word of that garbage you just gave me."

"But it's the truth!"

Alex made a snorting sound and began to pace in front of her desk. "Sure it is. That's why every time I've spoken to Kevin in the past few months, your name has been the one that keeps coming up." He stopped directly in front of her and glared. "Hell, he as much as told me two weeks ago that he was going to propose marriage to you."

Stunned, Desiree sank to her chair. "Kevin told you he was going to ask me to marry him?"

"No, not in those words precisely. But I realized once I got here and took stock of the situation that that's what he'd been trying to tell me."

"Why? What did he say?"

"It's not so much any one thing that he said, but several things he said. Add to that the reflective mood he was in and how his thoughts seemed to wander. Now I can see where he was heading with all that talk he was spouting about the importance of following one's dreams, of setting goals for the future and seeing them through."

Which explained why Kevin had upped and dashed off to Chicago the way he had, leaving her short one actor for her play and a weak promise to return in time for the opening. Kevin had gone in pursuit of his dreams—a deeper relationship with his girlfriend and a career on the stage.

Alex jammed his fingers through his hair, mussing the model-perfect cut and making him somehow more handsome because of it. "Fool that I am, at the time I thought he was talking about joining me at the firm."

Poor Alex. She could have told him that Kevin didn't have the least bit of interest in becoming an attorney or in joining the family-owned firm to run their megabusinesses.

"Of course, now I realize he was talking about *you* and his intention to marry you."

"What!" Desiree did a double take.

"Come off it, Ms. Mason. It all makes perfect sense now. Kevin was trying to tell me he wanted to marry you."

"And I'm beginning to think you're one beignet short of a dozen. Either that, or that Boston brain of yours can't handle the sky-high humidity down here. How on earth did you arrive at *that* ridiculous conclusion?"

"Quite easily, when you consider all the facts. First there's—"

"Stop!" Desiree raised her hand. "I don't even want to hear it. Kevin was not talking about marrying me. The dream he was referring to is his acting. He wants to be an actor, not an attorney." For now, she decided, it might be best to leave out the little detail of his dancer girlfriend.

"Don't be absurd. Kevin's not interested in acting. He's always wanted to be a lawyer."

"Then how do you explain the fact that he has a role in my play and that I met him while we were both working at another dinner theater?"

"If Kevin's shown any interest in acting recently, I'd say it's because of his involvement with you." Alex began to pace. "*You're* the one who's responsible for his quitting school."

"Now, wait a minute—"

"Damn." Alex slapped his palm with his fist. "I should have realized something was wrong when he came home a few weeks ago. He was quiet to the point of being somber. And Kevin is never somber."

No, he wasn't, Desiree admitted. Kevin was as happy-go-lucky as his brother was obviously serious.

"I should have known there was something behind all those crazy questions he was asking me."

"What crazy questions?"

Alex pinned her with his dark gaze. "Ridiculous questions like whether or not *I'd* ever been in love or if *I'd* ever thought about getting married."

Before she could check her reaction, Desiree asked, "What did you tell him?"

"No."

Of course, his answer would be no, Desiree decided. She didn't doubt for a minute that while Alexander Stone would probably be a generous lover, he would never give any woman his heart. For some reason she found that thought oddly depressing. "Well, I still don't see how Kevin's reflective mood and questions about *your* love life made you come to the conclusion that he was talking about marrying me."

Alex planted his hands on her desk and leaned forward, bringing his face eye level with hers. "It was simple. Because when I told Kevin that if he had any crazy ideas in his head about getting married he should forget them, he gave me that choirboy grin of his and told me not to worry. He said he'd already proposed to *you* and you had turned him down, claimed you were too old for him.'' Alex sneered. ''But I guess once you found out about his trust fund, a few years difference in age wasn't such a big problem anymore.''

Desiree lost it. She pushed to her feet and smacked her hands down on the desk. She leaned in, brought her face close to his, employing the same intimidation tactic he'd tried to use on her. Glaring at him, she said, ''You fool, I didn't even *know* Kevin had a trust fund. But if I did, it wouldn't have mattered a lick to me *if* I'd wanted to marry him. But I didn't. And I still don't. Kevin and I are friends. That's it. Just friends.''

''Then you don't deny that Kevin asked you to marry him?''

''No.'' Why should she? Kevin was a born flirt. He'd proposed to her and half of the females in the cast on a regular basis. No one took him seriously. No on except Alex, evidently.

The look Alex shot her could have withered a rock. ''Tell me, Ms. Mason, do all of your 'friends' go around asking you to marry them?''

She straightened her spine, tipped up her chin and did her best to look down her nose at him. ''No, not all of them,'' she replied sweetly, marveling at how she managed to sound so calm when inside she was spitting mad. She took pleasure in seeing the wariness creep into his eyes. ''Usually the only ones who propose marriage are the men.''

Three

Alex gritted his teeth. The woman was baiting him, and he knew it. He didn't doubt for a second that she had any number of men after her. Trouble was, he was hard-pressed not to join their ranks, because right now *he* wanted to pull her into his arms and kiss that sassy mouth of hers himself.

"But don't worry, Alex. If I ever decide to take Kevin up on his marriage proposal, you'll be among the first to know—right after we say 'I do.'" Tipping her chin up a notch, she gave him a chilly smile. "Now, you really will have to excuse me. I've got a dinner theater opening in just over a month, and I'm still short one cast member." She reached for the stack of business cards she'd been playing with a few minutes earlier. Sitting down in the chair behind the desk, she swiveled around and gave him her back.

Maybe it was several days of too little sleep. Maybe it

was the frustration of the morning's discoveries and being unable to locate Kevin. Or maybe it was just the simple fact that he'd been suffering with a bad case of lust from the moment he'd walked into that ballroom and seen this green-eyed siren about to marry a man he'd thought was his brother. Whatever the reason, her cool dismissal had done what few people, and certainly no woman, had had the power to do before. She'd destroyed the last of his control.

He didn't stop to think about how out of character his reactions to this woman were. He didn't stop to think how heavy-handed he was being. He didn't think period. Instead, he reacted.

In the space of a heartbeat, Alex was behind the desk, spinning her chair around so that she faced him. Grabbing the arms of the chair, he shoved it backward until the wheels hit the wall.

"Alex!"

He leaned forward, bringing his face so close to hers that he could see the black centers of her eyes widen in surprise, smell that damn flowered scent on her skin. "Maybe that duchess-to-peasant routine works on those college boys you're used to dealing with, but it doesn't work on me."

He heard her breath catch, watched the shock in her eyes fade and darken with awareness. The air hummed between them like an electrical wire that had snapped and was dangling dangerously during a storm. Her tongue slipped out to moisten her bottom lip. Alex's body hardened; blood rushed to his groin as he followed the movement.

"Tell me, Alexander Stone. Just what *does* work on you?"

Her husky, honeyed drawl set off images in his head

of satin sheets, soft skin and hot sex. His brain shut down as his body tightened with renewed desire. He stared at her slightly parted lips and gripped the arms of the chair even tighter. The need to taste that luscious mouth again hit him with the force of a prizefighter's fist. As though she could read his thoughts, her breath hitched. Her eyes fluttered closed.

Alex gave up and stopped fighting himself. He leaned a fraction closer, already anticipating the feel of her mouth beneath his, when suddenly something brushed against the back of his legs. He jerked away, nearly tumbled to the floor as he felt that "something" wind itself around his feet and legs. "What the—"

"Meow."

Alex glanced down at his feet where a black ball of fur was rubbing itself against his ankles, weaving its body in and out of his legs.

"Meow." The cat looked up at him and gave him another rub. Then it started to purr.

Alex wasn't sure whether he should curse the fur ball or thank it. He didn't have time to do either because his eyes began to water. Damn, he thought, blinking in reaction to the animal fur. But his allergy kicking in was a small price to pay, Alex told himself. If not for the cat's intervention, in another five seconds he would have been kissing Desiree.

That realization brought him up short. Alex scrubbed a hand over his face and shifted uncomfortably at the ache still present in his lower body. Lord, he'd been only a breath away from kissing her—a breath away from betraying his brother.

He winced at that sobering fact. Desiree Mason was by no means the first woman he'd ever wanted physically. There'd been several in his thirty-four years, and he'd enjoyed a number of satisfying sexual relationships with several of those women. But not one of those women had ever made him forget rhyme or reason. Not one of them had ever made him forget to put his brother's interests first.

Guilt slapped at him. What in heaven's name had he been thinking of? She was Kevin's girlfriend for Pete's sake! The woman Kevin thought he loved and wanted to marry.

And he wanted her for himself.

Disgusted with himself, Alex cut a glance to Desiree. He took in the sight of those tempting lips. She'd wanted him to kiss her, still wanted him to kiss her, judging by the dazed heat that lingered in her eyes. And heaven help him, he'd almost given in to the urge to do so, and would have, in fact, had it not been for the cat.

Alex clenched his jaw. For both his sake and Kevin's, he couldn't let his brother marry this woman, he told himself again. To do so would be a disaster. Somehow he had to find a way to prevent that from happening, because, despite her denials, he suspected her sights were set on his brother.

He could use himself as bait, a voice inside him whispered. He was rich, decent looking and wasn't without charm when the occasion called for it. Over the years he'd become adept at engaging in mutually satisfying relationships with women that never led to marriage. Why not do the same with Desiree? If he did, surely Kevin would see how wrong the woman was for him.

Alex frowned. The danger was he hadn't been thinking of Kevin or of saving his brother from Desiree's clutches when he'd almost kissed her. The truth was he hadn't been thinking at all.

The cat abandoned her dance around his legs and

jumped up to the credenza beside him, where it proceeded to nuzzle his arm, leaving a trail of black fur along the sleeve of his gray suit jacket. "Friend of yours?" Alex asked as he returned the cat to the floor only to have it promptly resume its perch beside him. Giving up, Alex moved out of the creature's path as his eyes started to fill again.

"That's Maggie," Desiree told him. Abandoning the chair, she walked over to the credenza and stooped down to face the cat. "Where have you been, you naughty girl? I was worried about you. I looked everywhere for you last night."

The cat meowed in response and licked at Desiree's outstretched fingers a moment before jumping down to the floor and heading straight for him. Alex's nose started to twitch as she brushed against his pant leg again.

"Maggie, what a shameless little flirt you are. Leave Alex alone and come back here."

The cat ignored Desiree and started in on the other leg of his suit trousers. Her silky black fur clung to the Armani like a magnet. Stepping over the cat, he removed himself as her rubbing post by walking over to the desk. The stubborn little fur ball trotted right behind him. The stinging in his eyes worsened. Alex blinked several times and reached for the handkerchief in his back pocket to wipe at his tearing eyes. "What's with this cat, anyway?"

"She likes men," Desiree offered by way of explanation.

Like mistress, like cat, Alex thought silently as his eyes continued to water and burn. His nose twitched again. Despite his efforts to control it, Alex gave in to the inevitable and sneezed.

"Bless you," Desiree said. Walking over to the desk,

she pulled open a drawer and withdrew a box of tissues. She shoved the box toward him.

"Thanks." Alex stuffed his handkerchief back into his pocket and snatched a handful of the tissues just before the next round of sneezing hit him.

After several moments the worst of the allergy attack was over. He wiped at his eyes again and watched as Desiree stooped down and retrieved Maggie. "Come on, sweetie. I think you're making poor Alex sneeze." She nuzzled the furry creature, heedless of the black fur it left clinging to her white shorts and blouse.

Alex stared at those long, slender fingers as she stroked the cat. Silently cursing himself, he tried to block out thoughts of what it would be like to have her fingers stroking him the same way.

Her hand went still at the sound of a tap on the door, and Alex breathed a prayer of thanks.

The tap sounded a second time. "Hey, Des. You in there?" The minister—minus his collar and robe—stuck his head in the door.

"Right here, Charlie."

The fellow stepped inside, then he looked from Desiree to him and back to Desiree again. "Sorry. Didn't mean to interrupt anything."

"You weren't. Mr. Stone and I were already finished our discussion. What's up?"

"That real estate lady, Miss Marilee, you know, the one with the fancy hats? She just called and said she's on her way over. She wants to pick up the key to the cottage. Says she's got a real hot prospect coming with her who might rent the place from you."

Alex didn't miss the look of hope that came into Desiree's eyes as she slid open a desk drawer and removed a ring with a gold-colored key.

"Well, let's hope Miss Marilee's right."

"Want me to wait out front for her and give her the key?" Charlie offered.

"Thanks, but I'll do it. You go on home." With the cat in her arms, Desiree started for the door.

"Ms. Mason. Desiree—" Alex began, only to sneeze again when she walked past him with the cat.

"Bless you."

"You getting sick?" Charlie asked. "Nothing worse than a summer cold."

"I don't believe that's a cold he's suffering from, Charlie," she said, pausing as the other man opened the door for her. "I have a strong suspicion that Mr. Stone here is allergic to cats," she said as she cuddled the ball of black fur in her arms.

"Pets," he corrected before sneezing again. "I'm allergic to pets period. It's the animal fur. And quit calling me Mr. Stone. My name's Alex."

The corners of her lips curved upward. "Well in that case, Alex, I'm sure you really don't want to spend any more time at Magnolia House than you already have."

Alex narrowed his still-tearing eyes. "I think I can manage to survive one little cat." That is, he could if he got some antihistamine tablets.

"Oh, but I wasn't referring to Maggie. I meant the rest of my little four-legged family."

"The rest?" he asked suspiciously, not liking the Cheshire Cat grin spreading across her lips.

"Uh-hmm. At last count, I believe there were thirteen of them."

"Thirteen! Nobody has thirteen cats!"

"Oh, but they're not all cats. Although I admit, several of them are Maggie's adorable siblings. I also have three dogs, a squirrel, a rabbit and—"

"Stop!" Alex held up his hand, his eyes filling again at just the thought of being subjected to all those animals—and the resulting bout of sneezing and weeping eyes.

She released a squirming Maggie, and the cat scooted out the door. "When you get back to Boston, you might want to see an allergist about some medication. Looks like you've got a bit of a rash starting on the side of your face."

Alex's hand went up to the right side of his face instinctively. He hadn't broken out with hives since he was a kid. At the twitch of her lips, he let his hand fall back to his side.

"And don't you worry. When Kevin gets back, I'll be sure to tell him that you came by." With a smug look on her face, she slipped out the door.

Frowning, Alex noted the seductive sway of her hips as she made her way down the hall with Maggie trotting at her heels.

"She's not kidding, you know."

Alex jerked his attention back to Charlie, the minister, who leaned against the doorway, an intent look on his face. "What was that?"

The older man folded his arms across his chest and gave him a measuring look. "I said she's not kidding about all those pets, so if you are allergic, you might want to take her advice and put some distance between you and this place."

"I'll keep it in mind."

The other guy shrugged. "Suit yourself. But if you hang around here you're liable to run into more than a few of Desiree's critters. She's got herself a whole mess of them. Cats, dogs, even a squirrel just like she said. Doesn't matter what it is, if the creature shows up here on her property, the next thing you know, she's given the thing a name and made it a part of her family.''

"She sounds like a veterinarian's dream.''

Charlie's lips kicked up in a half smile. "Yeah. I suspect she is.''

Which was one more reason Kevin and his trust fund would be attractive to her. He had friends who claimed to spend a fortune on only one pet; he could imagine the tab for thirteen. With the cat gone, his breathing was becoming somewhat easier, Alex realized. Now he just had to get rid of the fur Maggie had left behind. Tossing the soiled tissues into the trash, he began brushing at the black hair on his jacket and pants.

"So, you planning to stick around?'' Charlie asked.

Alex looked up at the other man. "I might be. You have a problem with that?''

"Depends on your reason for sticking around. That Desiree, she's a real sweet kid. Sometimes too sweet for her own good. She's got this tendency to take in strays—both the two-legged and four-legged variety, if you know what I mean.''

He understood all right. "You mean she's a soft touch.'' Which surprised him, given her profession as an actress and her latching onto his brother.

Charlie rubbed at his jaw, looking less and less like a minister and more and more like a papa bear guarding his cub. "I guess that's how some people would see her. Me? I see a beautiful woman with a generous heart. Sometimes that big heart of hers gets her into trouble.''

"I bet.'' If Charlie was to be believed, the woman was a cross between a saint and Mother Teresa. But he didn't recall any of the nuns from his grade-school days looking like Desiree Mason. He thought of that heart-shaped mole on her shoulder, the way she'd trembled when he had touched her. He had a hard time tagging Desiree as the naive woman Charlie described when just looking at her had his brain shutting down and his body aching for her in his bed.

Irritated with himself, Alex gave up on getting rid of the cat hair and started for the door. He stopped when Charlie put his short, round body in his path. "Was there something else?" Alex asked.

The older man tipped his head back and met Alex's gaze. "Every now and then one of those strays Desiree takes in turns real nasty, even bites the hand that feeds it. I'd hate to see Desiree get bitten because she mistook some wolf for another helpless stray."

"You can quit worrying. I'm not helpless and I have no intention of becoming one of Desiree's strays. I'm only interested in one thing—and that's making sure my brother doesn't screw up his life by dropping out of law school and rushing into a relationship he isn't ready for."

"So you're saying your only interest in Desiree is in her relationship with your brother?"

"Yes," Alex assured him. "That's exactly what I'm saying."

"Then how come when I came in here the air between you two was as steamy as the swamp in July?"

"Because we didn't see eye to eye about her relationship with my brother."

"That's the reason, when you watched her walk out of here, you had the look of a man that's been in the desert for a long, long time without any water and has just stumbled on a cool mountain stream?"

Alex nearly winced at the man's analogy. It was a good one and was closer to the mark that he'd like to admit. Had he been so transparent that even a stranger could see how much he had wanted her? "I don't know what you think you saw, pal. But I can tell you, my only interest in Desiree Mason is in her connection to my brother.''

Charlie eyed him skeptically. ''Kevin's not here. He's out of town.''

''So I've been told. Do you know where he went?''

The other man shook his head. ''Nope. But he promised Desiree he'd be back in time for the play's opening.''

''Then he really is in the play?'' Alex asked, surprised.

''Sure. He's got to do the role that we thought *you* were substituting for today—the part of the brother who stops the wedding.''

''And he's supposed to be back for the opening? You're sure about that.''

''That's what he said.''

Alex chewed on that bit of information and tried for more. ''Exactly when is this play supposed to open?''

''Next month. In time for the July Fourth weekend.''

''Thanks, Charlie. You've been a big help.''

And as Alex exited Magnolia House and got into his rental car, he pointed the car in the direction of the cottage he'd spotted earlier.

Since Desiree refused to tell him where Kevin was, and no one else seemed quite sure where he'd gone, he'd simply wait for his brother to return. Pulling the car to a stop, he punched out the number on the sign of the realty agency listing the rental property. ''Miss Marilee Simmons, please. I'd like to speak to her about renting the cottage she has listed on Magnolia Lane.''

''Well, sweetie, it looks like we're going to be able to keep you and your brothers in cat food after all,'' Desiree told Maggie. Holding the kitten up to eye level she looked into its gold-green eyes. "Miss Marilee finally rented the cottage for us."

Maggie meowed in response.

"This calls for a celebration, don't you think? What do you say we skip the Nine Lives tonight and open up a couple of cans of tuna fish instead. Would you like that?"

The little cat's pink tongue darted out and flicked the tip of Desiree's nose. She laughed and cuddled the cat to her breast. "I take it that was a yes."

Maggie's little engine started to run, and Desiree settled back in the chair at her desk. As she stroked the cat's silky black fur, she went back to reviewing the ad copy scheduled to run in the newspaper announcing the dinner theater's opening next month. Her stomach knotted as she looked at the accompanying bill for the advertising spread. "Thank heavens Marilee did rent that cottage," she said. The money from the rental couldn't have come at a better time.

It still amazed her at just how costly her dream of turning Magnolia House into a dinner theater was proving to be. Not that she hadn't been warned. Her sister Clea had tried to tell her it wouldn't be easy when she'd co-signed the loan for her to buy the place. Desiree frowned, still disliking the fact that she'd had to have a guarantor. But according to the bank her occupation as an actress—even one who'd once worked on Broadway, albeit only for two months—wasn't considered a good financial risk. Not that she blamed them. Most of her jobs had been temporary, including the ones she'd taken over the years to supplement her acting income. Evidently her two-month run in a Broadway production didn't paint a picture of stability when they included her off-off-Broadway performances, dozen-plus waitressing positions and the disastrous four-week stint as a veterinarian's assistant. It was a good thing her nose-to-the grindstone, financial whiz, older sister had come to the rescue. Otherwise, she'd never have been able to buy the place.

Her hand stilled in the middle of scratching Maggie's ear as she read the staggering fee for a two-page spread in the newspaper and the pitiful discount being offered if she ran the ad for two consecutive weeks. Desiree sighed and reached for her pen. If Magnolia House was going to succeed, it had to be done, she told herself, as she checked off the block for two weeks of advertising. And Magnolia House *would* succeed, she vowed silently. She couldn't afford for it to do otherwise—not with her sister on the hook to the bank with her for the money she'd borrowed.

Tossing down the pen, she turned her chair to look out the window. Magnolia trees stretched along the road as far as the eye could see, their branches heavy with white blossoms and shiny, dark green leaves. She stared past the road to the wildflowers of bright yellow and orange that swayed under the kiss of a summer breeze and smiled as her gaze shifted to the lake and gazebo in the distance.

Home, she thought as her eyes roamed the landscape. She felt warmed by the knowledge that this beautiful place belonged to her—even if the bank did have first dibs on it. She chuckled at the thought of herself as not only a single homeowner, but a businesswoman to boot. Who could have predicted such a thing? Surely not her parents or her sisters. She'd been the last person anyone would have expected to become an entrepreneur—including her. Having led a gypsy-like childhood, due to her parents' work as movie extras and the nine nomadic years she'd spent since leaving the nest moving to wherever the roles took her, she'd never dreamed she'd ever *want* to be a businesswoman tied to one place.

She'd certainly never considered actually buying a home—at least not one to live in alone. Sure, she'd always envisioned settling down someday, but never like this. Never without falling in love first, getting married and selecting that perfect home with her husband by her side.

And then she'd taken that wrong turn while en route to meet some fellow actors at a boat festival on the north shore of New Orleans and had stumbled upon Magnolia House. It had been love at first sight for her. She'd known at once that the old, abandoned plantation house with its ancient trees and gazebo was the one place she wanted to stay.

Sighing, Desiree turned back to the ledger of expenses and the dwindling balance that remained from the loan. At the time, she'd thought it so much money, more than she could ever need to get the place in shape and launch it as a dinner theater. But, as usual, Clea had been right. Renovations were expensive, but starting up a business was even more so. Thank heavens her sister had insisted she budget for unexpected things like the death of the oven in the main kitchen the previous month. Only, who would have thought the new model would cost even more than she'd anticipated and force her to cut into her advertising funds?

But now the rental fee for the cottage would replace that money and even give her a little extra. Desiree smiled. Renting the gardener's cottage had been a stroke of genius on Kevin's part. Since she had no gardener and no intention of getting one, renting the place made perfect sense. And the rental fee would enable her to do the full-blown advertising blitz she'd planned for Magnolia

House's grand opening. She would have to thank Kevin for coming up with the idea as soon as he returned.

And she'd also have to tell him about Alex's visit. Memories of her encounter with Alex the previous day came back to her in a rush. She could still see him racing down the aisle of the mock chapel, so tall and handsome with his dark hair and those oh-so-serious midnight eyes. He looked like he'd stepped out of the pages of a romance novel.

Her pulse picked up speed as she remembered the feel of his hands, warm and hard, on her skin, the sight of his black eyes growing even darker as he'd stared at her mouth, the whisper of his breath on her lips as he'd leaned closer. She pressed her fingertips to her lips. Sweet mercy, but she had wanted him to kiss her.

And what a mistake it would have been if he had, she assured herself. The man had been far too quick to jump to conclusions about her and his brother. Perhaps she had made matters worse by egging him on, letting him believe that she and Kevin were engaged, but he'd deserved it for his smug assumption that she was after Kevin's money.

She was lucky. She'd dodged the proverbial bullet yesterday, she told herself. Thanks to Maggie and his allergic reaction to the little darling, she'd gotten rid of him before she'd made a complete idiot of herself. She gave the snoozing kitten a tiny squeeze. "I owe you bunches for scaring him off."

Desiree glanced up as a car turned onto the far end of the road leading to Magnolia House. She followed its progress, a part of her half expecting and half wanting Alex to show up again.

Ridiculous, she chided herself. He was probably already back in Boston by now. Besides she'd have to be crazy or have a death wish to want him to come back. The car started down the drive leading to the house. Pushing thoughts of Alex from her mind, Desiree smiled as she recognized Marilee's white Cadillac.

"Hello, Marilee," Desiree greeted the real estate agent a few minutes later.

"Hello, dear." Marilee tucked a strand of ash blond hair into place with one hand before extending her hand. Desiree eyed the older woman's periwinkle silk dress and matching hat and couldn't help noting that they were almost the exact shade as her eyes. A true Southern belle, Desiree thought, marveling that the fifty-plus woman seemed to have the energy of a woman half her age. "I've got the lease right here in my briefcase," she said, patting the slim burgundy leather valise. "As soon as your new tenant arrives and gives me his check for two months' rent, I'll have you sign the lease and give you the agency's check less our commission. Do you want to look over the lease before he gets here?"

"Not unless I need to. I mean, you did say it was all pretty standard, didn't you?"

"And it is."

"Then, I'll trust you to make sure that everything's in order. Just tell me where I need to sign when the time comes." Desiree returned to her seat at the desk, and Maggie immediately jumped up into her lap. "I still can't believe you were able to rent the cottage. I mean, the place has been listed for more than four months, and we've only had three people even want to see it."

The other woman beamed. "Salesmanship, Desiree, my dear. It's simply a question of salesmanship. Let's face it. Your little cottage, sweet though it is, has its drawbacks. After all, it's an hour's drive from here to the city. But as I've pointed out to my clients with car phones and even faxes making everyone so much more accessible, the commute in exchange for life in the country is not a bad trade-off.''

Desiree cut a glance to her left as a black Lexus turned onto the road and headed toward the house. For some reason her stomach fluttered with anticipation, and she had to force her attention back to Marilee.

''And who wouldn't want to wake up to such a magnificent view?'' Marilee spread her hands, indicating the grounds that lay beyond the window.

When Desiree looked at the road again, the car had disappeared from her line of vision, its driver evidently already at the front door of Magnolia House.

''I mean, there's not only this grand house to rest one's eyes upon each morning, but the grounds are simply wonderful, all those magnolia trees, that little lake and gazebo. Why, Mr. Stone didn't even balk when I insisted he had to sign a six-month lease.''

Desiree's heart suddenly did a frantic two-step. Her stomach fell. ''Mr. Stone?'' She leaned forward, gripping the edge of the desk. ''A Mr. Stone is the person who rented the cottage?''

Marilee tipped her head to one side and gave her a curious look. ''Why, yes. A very nice gentleman he is. And a handsome one, too.''

It couldn't be, Desiree told herself, even knowing it was a lie. ''What's his first name, Marilee?'' she asked anyway.

''I...umm. Arnold, I think. No. that doesn't sound right. Was it Adam? No, that's not right, either.'' She flicked the lock open on her briefcase. ''I'm afraid I'm just hopeless when it comes to names. Let me take a look at the lease.'' She pulled out the papers, scanned them. ''Yes, here it is. Your new tenant's name is—''

''Stone. Alexander Stone,'' Alex replied from the doorway.

Four

"**N**o!" Desiree shot to her feet, her raised voice and abrupt movement causing Maggie to leap to the floor. "I'm not renting the cottage to you!"

"Is there a problem?" Alex asked innocently, giving Maggie a wide berth as she raced past him out of the room.

"You bet there's a problem. I don't want *you* as a tenant."

Marilee made a strangled sound, and for a moment Desiree half expected the other woman to faint.

"Why not?" Alex asked.

"Because I—" Scrambling, Desiree stared at him in disbelief. She'd been attracted to him, and the stupid man had all but accused her of being some kind of gold digger with designs on his younger brother. "You *know* why."

"I assume you're referring to our little misunderstanding earlier."

"Misunderstanding?" Marilee said, her gaze swinging back and forth between the two of them, causing her wide-brimmed hat to tip slightly.

"I'm afraid I foolishly jumped to some inaccurate conclusions yesterday and in doing so I offended Ms. Mason," Alex explained smoothly. "It was a mistake for which I'm truly sorry."

Sorry, my eye, Desiree thought. There had been no misunderstanding. He'd been all too clear in his opinion of her, and she didn't think for a moment he'd changed his mind, either.

Marilee waved her hand. "We all make mistakes, Mr. Stone. I'm sure Desiree understands and accepts your apology. There's no reason at all why you can't rent the cottage. All I need from you now is your check."

"No," Desiree countered, irritated that, even now, just looking at the way his oxford shirt stretched over those Viking shoulders of his could still make her pulse hammer. Only a complete idiot would set herself up for that kind of fall, she told herself. And she might have a romantic streak in her, but she was no idiot. "I'm not going to lease him the cottage."

"Of course you are, dear," Marilee replied in a strained voice. "Mr. Stone's already signed the lease. Now, if I could just have your check, Mr. Stone."

"I said no."

The agent gave her a brittle smile. "Really, Desiree. Mr. Stone has already apologized for the little misunderstanding the two of you had yesterday, and he wants to rent the cottage. I can't imagine that you could still have a problem leasing it to him."

"But I do have a problem leasing him the cottage."

"Well, what on earth is it?"

"Yes, Desiree, what is the problem?" Alex asked. Desiree caught the challenge in his eyes. The problem was the man was trouble with a capital *T*. Not for a single minute did she trust him or his motives for wanting to rent her cottage. "The problem is that Mr. Stone's an attorney, and I don't like attorneys."

Marilee made a choking sound. Managing a tight smile, she said, "Really, dear, that's not a very good reason. I mean, Mr. Stone here meets all the terms you specified in a tenant. His references checked out perfectly. He's agreed to lease the cottage for the six months you required and to pay the first and last month's rent in advance just as the lease stipulates. To refuse him simply on the basis that he's an attorney, that would be...well, it could easily be construed as discrimination on your part."

"Then let him sue me."

The agent frowned. "Actually, he could. It would be well within his rights. And, well, to be perfectly honest, my agency probably would sue you, as well. The contract you signed with us clearly states that if we find a suitable tenant, one that meets all your requirements and ours, and you refuse to rent to that tenant without just cause, then you're liable for the full commission the agency would have earned for the lease had you accepted it."

Quickly Desiree tallied the commission Marilee was talking about and nearly cringed. No way could she afford to pay *that* kind of money without the income from the rental. And judging from the woman's determined expression, Marilee Simmons had no intention of walking out that door without getting her full commission. "But I don't *want* to lease it to him," Desiree insisted. "I want you to find me another tenant."

"There's nothing wrong with *this* tenant."

"I've already told you. I don't want to lease it to him."

Marilee shook her head. "I'm afraid you'll need a better reason than the one you've given for refusing to lease him the cottage.''

Desiree glared at Alex for putting her in this spot to begin with. She spun around, unable to think with those midnight eyes of his watching her. She had to figure a way out of this mess. It was bad enough that she'd been on the verge of making a complete fool of herself with the man yesterday. What would it be like if she rented him the cottage? She didn't believe for a second that he'd changed his mind about her. He probably still believed she was involved with his brother.

And what about Kevin? What would happen when he came back? What if Kevin came back engaged? If Alex was right in his assessment of Kevin's mood and comments, it was certainly possible. She didn't even want to think about how Alex would react to that bit of news. And what about Kevin's part in her show? He'd promised to be back in plenty of time for the opening. Suppose Alex convinced Kevin to abandon his dream of acting and return with him to Boston? Where would that leave her for the opening? She still hadn't come up with anyone who was even close to being as good as Kevin in the role.

"Desiree? Do you have any valid reason why you can't lease the cottage to Mr. Stone?" Marilee asked.

She turned around to face the agent. "Yes. I've...I've changed my mind about renting the cottage. I don't want to rent it after all.''

"Oh, my. I'm afraid you've put me in an awkward position, my dear. You see, you signed a six-month contract with my agency to lease the cottage for you. That contract doesn't expire for another two months and well, it's the agency's policy not to terminate contracts before the expiration date. A lot of time, money and effort have already been expended by my firm and me, personally, on your behalf to fulfill that contract. We've done our job. We've found you an acceptable tenant, one who meets all of your requirements and the terms of the lease. So, despite the fact that you may have changed your mind about wanting to lease the cottage, unless you're prepared to pay my firm its full commission, I'm afraid you'll have to honor our contract and lease the cottage to Mr. Stone.''

Oh, how did I ever let myself get into this mess? She looked down at the lease on her desk waiting for her signature and stared at the dates of the lease. If she signed the darned thing, Alex would have use of the cottage from now through December. How was she going to—

Suddenly an idea struck her. ''Actually, there's another problem, Marilee. I'm afraid I made a mistake about the length of the lease. I realize I can't possibly accept a six-month lease on the cottage from Mr. Stone or anyone. It would have to be a year's lease with the entire year's rent paid in advance or I simply can't lease it.''

Marilee sucked in her breath. ''Honestly, Desiree. You can't make a change like that at this stage—not when we've already found you a tenant. Besides, no one in his right mind would ever agree to such terms.''

''Well, those are the only terms under which I'm going to agree to lease it.''

''Done.''

''You can't—'' Marilee swung her gaze toward Alex. ''What did you say?''

''I agree to Ms. Mason's terms. I'll lease the cottage for a year and pay her the full year's rent in advance.'' He reached for his checkbook and pen. ''Who should I make the check out to?''

Marilee happily told him. And while Desiree tried to recover from the swift turn of events, Alex scribbled the enormous sum across the face of a check and signed his name to it. He glanced up at her as he tore the check from the book and handed it to Marilee. His eyes held the satisfied gleam of a warrior who'd just tasted victory. "I'd like to move in this afternoon, if that's OK."

Desiree remained speechless as Marilee amended the lease terms and had Alex initial the pages. Then she turned to her. "All right, dear. All I need now is for you to sign the lease and initial the changes where I've indicated. And here's your check for the year's lease paid in full, less my commission."

She glanced at the large sum of money written across the face of the check, then shifted her gaze to the advertising bill lying on her desk beside the lease. Still she hesitated. She'd be a fool not to take it, she told herself. She could certainly use the money to help with the dinner theater kick-off and put the rest of it away for the future. Besides, not for a second did she honestly believe Alex would stay for an entire year. A week, maybe two weeks tops, she figured. Surely by then Kevin would be back. Then one way or another, with or without his brother, Alex would leave and go back to Boston.

"Go ahead and sign it, Desiree," Alex urged her.

She stared at him for long moments, her pulse quickening as she remembered the impulsive kiss she'd given him at the rehearsal and how close she'd come to kissing him a second time in this very room yesterday.

"Unless, of course, there's another, more personal reason that you're worried about having me around."

Desiree caught the note of amusement in his voice and was sure he knew she'd been remembering what had passed between them yesterday. And the dratted man knew exactly how he had affected her. Irritated with herself and him, she snatched the pen he held out to her and signed her name to the lease. She handed it to Marilee. Quickly the agent dispensed one copy to her and another one to Alex, then made a fast exit, leaving her alone with Alex.

"I don't know why you leased the cottage, but if you did it with the intention of trying to break up a romance between me and Kevin, I'm afraid you've just thrown away a lot of money for nothing." She waved the check before him. Folding it, she tucked it in the pocket of her skirt. "Because there is no romance between me and Kevin."

"So you've said."

"It's true."

"I didn't say it wasn't."

But for the life of her, Desiree didn't think he believed her. He picked up a photo of her and her two sisters from her desk. Desiree snatched it from his fingers and set it back down on the desk. "If your intention isn't to try to break up a nonexistent romance between me and your brother, then why did you rent the cottage?"

"As I told Miss Simmons, I want a little getaway place in the country."

"You live in Boston," she reminded him. "I'm sure you could find any number of little country getaways a lot closer to home than this."

He smiled, and Desiree felt the impact of that killer grin all the way to her toes. "True. There are quite a few beautiful country places in Massachusetts, but there's nothing quite like this. Nothing with this feel of the South. I think your little cottage will be a perfect place for me to get away and relax."

"But you're not actually planning to stay here, right? I mean aside from an occasional weekend, you'll be going back to Boston." If he was only going to be around for a couple of days now and then, surely she could manage to avoid him for those few days that he'd be here.

"Eventually."

"Eventually?" she repeated, growing more suspicious by the moment.

"I realized yesterday that it's been a long time since I've taken a vacation. I thought maybe I'd take a few weeks off and enjoy your Southern countryside."

Desiree narrowed her eyes. According to Kevin, his brother *never* took time off from work. It was one of the reasons the firm had doubled in size under Alex's direction and opened branches in several major cities and Europe—not to mention the other chunk of businesses he owned. And hadn't Kevin told her that even the women in Alex's life—and she didn't doubt for a second that there had been a number of them, considering his looks and money—took a back seat when it came to Alex's business? "What about your businesses?" she asked.

"One of the perks of being the owner is that I can set my own work schedule."

Desiree frowned. "But who's going to run your…your conglomerate while you're down here soaking up the Louisiana countryside?"

He arched his brow. "My conglomerate?"

She flushed. "Kevin said you were a very successful businessman and that you had a lot of interests besides the law firm."

"Yes, I suppose that's true. It's one of the reasons I'd wanted Kevin to get his law degree. I'd hoped he would be able to help me run the operation."

It made sense, and she didn't doubt he had Kevin's best interests at heart. Still, it was obviously not what Kevin wanted. "And if that's not what Kevin wants, if he's not interested in being a lawyer or in running those businesses, what then?"

"Then I'd be disappointed and hope I could change his mind."

"He wants to be an actor."

"He's too young to know what he wants to do with his life at this point. But it's not Kevin I'm interested in discussing right now."

He moved around the desk to stand in front of her, and Desiree fought the urge to step back. His scent, a combination of woods and soap and male, surrounded her. When his eyes darkened and his gaze fell to her lips, her heart stammered. Squeezing the ring with the cottage key on it that she'd been holding in her hand, she shoved it at Alex. "Here's the key to the cottage."

Alex took the key from her fingers but held on to her hand, sending her pulse into overdrive. "Aren't you going to give me a tour of the grounds?"

Desiree pulled her hand free. "Sorry. No time. I have a lot of work to do this afternoon. If you'd like, I'll ask Charlie to take you around when he gets here."

"That's all right," he said, a knowing grin curving his lips. "It can wait for another time when you're not so busy."

"Damn!" Alex threw down the razor he'd picked up at a quaint little country store the previous evening and pressed his fingers to the stinging nick on his chin. After a moment he rinsed off the remainder of the shaving cream and blotted his face dry. Turning his head slightly, he dabbed at the nick once more with a tissue before slapping on some of the aftershave he'd purchased along with the razor. He studied the results in the ancient mirror and sighed. It would have to do, he told himself, at least until the things he'd instructed his assistant to send him arrived.

After running a comb through his hair, he pulled on the khaki slacks, shirt and dock shoes he'd purchased. Not his usual style, he admitted. But then, somehow he didn't think the suit he'd worn when he'd arrived two days ago would stand up to another day of this incessant heat.

"Just my luck to get stuck in this town in the midst of a heat wave," he muttered. When he'd decided to come to New Orleans, he hadn't planned to be here for more than a few hours at best—just long enough to talk some sense into his brother. But then he hadn't anticipated not finding Kevin when he got here. He certainly hadn't planned on finding himself leasing Desiree Mason's cottage for a year. And he positively hadn't planned on finding himself attracted to the woman.

Attracted, he scoffed silently. It was a mild description for his reaction to her. He recalled the sight of that redgold hair falling decadently around her bare shoulders, of how he'd itched to catch it in his hands, wrap the silky length around his fists while his mouth worked its way up her slender throat to taste those pouty lips. Growing aroused at just the thought of her, Alex swore again and strode from the room. The idea had been to discourage the little witch's interest in his brother, not to fall for her himself.

Evidently, his self-imposed sabbatical on relationships with the female sex had been too long if this hungering for Desiree Mason was any indication. The woman wasn't even his type, he reminded himself as he made his way through the cottage to the living room. Yet, there was no denying the fact that he wanted her. He'd tossed and turned most of the night just thinking about her. And his restlessness hadn't had a thing to do with his brainstorm yesterday to set himself up as a target to deflect any designs she had on Kevin. Considering his own response to the woman, that scheme didn't have a prayer.

No, while he waited for Kevin, he'd be far wiser keeping his distance from the lady. Maybe she had been telling the truth about her relationship with Kevin. But it wouldn't hurt to learn a bit more about her, he reasoned, and made a mental note to have a background check run on her.

Pushing images of Desiree from his mind, he forced himself to focus on business. He thought of the Harrison contracts waiting on his desk back in Boston and flexed his fingers, eager to pick up the phone and have his assistant fax the documents to him. Problem was, he didn't have a fax machine yet, and the blasted phone line still hadn't been connected.

Walking into the kitchen, he went straight for the copper canisters on the wooden shelf and retrieved the one marked Coffee. He opened it and grimaced. Empty. His stomach grumbled for the third time that morning, reminding him dinner had been a long time ago. After a check of the refrigerator netted a six-pack of colas, a bottle of white wine and a tray of ice cubes, Alex shut the door and sighed. He'd have to make a run to the grocery store to stock up on food sometime today. But first he had to find a cup of coffee and a telephone. So much for keeping his distance from Desiree. Telling himself it was an emergency of sorts, he swiped the door key from the table and set off for Magnolia House.

He had to admit, Alex told himself as he made his way down the winding road past the lake to the main house, the place really was pleasant. At least it was in the morning hours before the heat and humidity reached its peak. A pair of squirrels scampered across the road and scurried up an oak tree. To his left a calico cat stalked a sparrow in the branches of another magnificent oak. Alex shook his head as he recalled Desiree's claim about the pets. Despite the fact that he'd picked up some over-the-counter antihistamines after his encounter with Maggie, he'd just as soon steer clear of the rest of her four-legged friends.

He climbed up the stairs and knocked on the door. It swung open under the pressure of his fist. Stepping inside, he wasn't the least bit surprised to find the reception desk once again empty. Unsure where to find Desiree to ask about coffee and the use of a phone, he decided to check her office first. He stopped after no more than a few steps, his attention snagged by the sound of voices. Changing direction, he followed the rumble of voices and the tantalizing aroma of fresh coffee and frying bacon.

Alex sniffed. His mouth watered as he entered what appeared to be a small dining room. The place was filled with people—many of whom he recognized from the wedding scene rehearsal two days earlier. Only now, instead of wearing black ties and bridesmaid dresses, they were in shorts and T-shirts, and busily scoffing down what appeared to be mountains of bacon and eggs.

The door to his left swung open and Alex jumped back as Desiree sauntered out, carrying a platter piled high with biscuits. Alex sucked in his breath. All thoughts about how close she'd come to plowing him down with the door, even at how good those biscuits had smelled when she went by, flew right out of his head as he took in the pair of long, slender legs and swaying hips. Reminding himself to breathe, Alex ran his gaze up the length of those incredible legs, over the brief white shorts and yellow blouse. He noted the hair pulled up on top of her head, the red-gold wisps trailing lazily down the back of her neck. Desire licked through him with the piercing heat of a blowtorch, making him ache.

"Here you go, guys," Desiree said as she plopped down the dish of flaky biscuits. Hands came from all directions, and the pile disappeared almost immediately. She laughed. "You'd better enjoy them. Harry said that's the last batch you're getting this morning."

She was still smiling when she turned around and spotted him. Her smile wavered and after a moment's hesitation, she started toward him. Alex's gut tightened as he noted the way her blouse cupped the curve of her breasts and dipped in at her waist.

"Good morning, Counselor. You're up early."

"Morning," he finally managed to get the words past his too dry throat.

Silence hung in the air between them for long moments. "I trust you found everything you needed last night at the cottage?"

He tried to think, to remember what he'd wanted to ask her, but his mind had gone blank at the sight of her.

She tipped her head to the side, gave him a wary look. "Was there something you needed?"

Alex shook his head, trying to regain control of himself. "Yes, I...I was wondering if I could use the phone and maybe get a cup of coffee. I haven't had a chance to get any supplies yet."

His stomach chose that moment to grumble, and Desiree laughed. "Sounds to me like you're in need of more than just a cup of coffee. Would you like some breakfast?"

"I didn't realize you were open for breakfast."

"I'm not."

"But all those people," he indicated with the tilt of his head in the direction of the tables.

"Oh, they're not customers," she informed him with a wave of her hand. "Some of them are employees, some are neighbors. But most of them are just guys from the cast. We have a rehearsal scheduled for later this morning. They just decided to come a bit early."

Alex cut a glance to the man he recognized as O'Reilly, her groom, and watched him slather his biscuit with butter and jelly. "And you're feeding all of them breakfast and not charging them for it?"

"Charge them? Why on earth would I charge them for a bite of breakfast? Those people are my friends," she insisted as though that explained it all.

He'd suspected she'd leased the cottage because of strained finances. If she fed this group for nothing on a regular basis, he could certainly understand why she'd have trouble making ends meet. Either she was a lousy businesswoman or the biggest soft touch he'd ever met. "Just how often does this sort of thing happen?"

She squinched her brows together and stared at him as though *he* was the one who was crazy. "How often does what happen?" she asked in a voice that reflected how strange she found the question.

"These friends of yours showing up for a free meal."

She hiked her chin up a notch, and despite the fact that he had a good six inches on her in height, she managed to do a good job of looking down her nose at him. "I don't know how things are done back in Boston, but in the South we don't charge our friends for a little hospitality."

Judging from her reaction, he'd bet it was a regular occurrence. Which was one more reason Kevin and his trust fund would be attractive to her. The lady was going to need a chunk of cash if this was the way she intended to operate her dinner theater.

"Do you or don't you want some breakfast?"

"I do. And, Desiree?" She paused and looked at him out of stormy green eyes. "Thanks." If she could feed that crew, he reasoned, as he followed her into the kitchen, one more free meal wasn't going to matter much at this point. Besides, he had a difficult enough time thinking straight when he was around the woman. With a bit of luck, he might be able to think more clearly on a full stomach.

"Have a seat," she told him, pointing to a table and

two chairs set in a breakfast nook that looked out over an orchard of fig trees. "I'll be right back."

Alex took a seat and watched as she went over to the stove. She wrapped her arms around a big, beefy man sporting a mess of tattoos on biceps and forearms the size of tree trunks.

"Cut that nonsense out, girl," the fellow grumbled.

"Now, Harry, is that any way to speak to the woman who loves you?" Alex watched with a mixture of envy and curiosity as she planted a smacking kiss on the guy's cheek.

A flush climbed up the man's neck to spread across his face and bald head. "I told you to cut that out." He grabbed the end of a splattered apron that Alex suspected had once been white and rubbed at the lipstick on his cheek. "Now look what you've done. How am I gonna explain that lipstick on my apron to Mona?"

Desiree smiled. "You'll just have to tell her the truth. That I threw myself at you and you rejected me…again."

The old guy grunted, but a half grin snuck its way across his stern mouth. "All right. What is it you want this time? More biscuits? Bacon?"

Desiree whispered something in his ear and he nodded. "All right. Go on, then. Get out of my way. I'll let you know when it's ready."

Ignoring his scowl, she gave him another smack on his cheek, then made her way over to the pot of coffee. She poured two cups, topped them off with steaming milk and sauntered back to the table to join Alex.

"You're in luck," she told him as she placed one of the cups before him. She slipped into the chair across from him. "Harry's agreed to cook us some grits and eggs."

Alex arched his brow. "You mean that little performance a minute ago was just to get him to cook me breakfast?''

''Actually,'' she said, a wide grin curving her mouth. ''That was to get him to fix *both* of us breakfast. I haven't eaten yet and I'm starving.'' She picked up her coffee, took a sip and sighed. ''Hmm. There is nothing like New Orleans coffee.''

Alex eyed the cup in front of him. Instead of the rich, black brew he was accustomed to, this stuff looked more like weak tea.

''Taste it,'' she encouraged him. ''It's café au lait— coffee with milk.''

''I drink my coffee black.''

''You're in Louisiana, Alex,'' she chided as though he were a small child. ''No one drinks their coffee black in New Orleans.''

''We're not in New Orleans,'' he pointed out. ''This is Madisonville.''

She wrinkled her nose. ''We're just across the lake. Go ahead. Try it. The coffee has chicory in the blend. It's really strong. That's why it's served with steamed milk—to cut the bite.''

He had to admit, the stuff did smell wonderful. ''How is it you know so much about the customs here? Kevin said you were from the West Coast.''

She arched her brow. ''I guess you remembered that because of that super brain of yours. Kevin said you were very smart. A genius, in fact.''

Alex flushed at the mention of his IQ. Evidently Kevin had seen fit to tell Desiree more about him than he'd thought. ''Is that your way of avoiding my question?''

''Not at all.'' Desiree grinned. ''Actually, I was born in Chicago, but I did live on the West Coast for a while just before I moved here. I've also lived in at least half of the states at one time or another. But this is the only place I ever decided I wanted to stay. It's certainly the only place I ever bought a home. I guess I sort of adopted the place and it adopted me. Anyway, I love it here."

And the lady looked right at home, he thought, as he stirred the coffee in front of him and contemplated taking a sip.

"Go ahead. Give it a try. If you don't like it, I'll get you another cup without milk. But I'm warning you, once you've had your coffee this way, you'll never go back to having it plain again."

And she had been right. By the time he'd finished his third cup of coffee and eaten one of the finest breakfasts he'd ever tasted, he'd almost forgotten his reason for coming here in the first place.

He'd also forgotten his promise to himself to keep his distance from Desiree. What still puzzled him was his attraction to her. He'd always been drawn to attractive, cultured women—women who knew how to dress, who were conversant in business, who served on the boards of the right charitable and social committees, who could trace their bloodlines back to the Mayflower or sometimes even royalty.

Yet, here she was with her face free of makeup, her feet bare, talking about off-off-Broadway plays and parents who trailed around after B-movie productions and he found himself fascinated. Worse, the sexual pull he'd sensed between them was twice as strong as it had been the previous day. He wanted to reach across the table and taste her tempting mouth to see if it was as tantalizing as he remembered. He wrapped his hands around his coffee cup instead.

"You finished with that cup or you planning to strangle it some more?"

Alex blinked and looked up at the tattooed muscle man masquerading as a cook. The guy looked more like a prizefighter than a chef, he thought. He set down the cup. "I'm finished. Thank you for the breakfast. Everything was excellent."

The fellow merely grunted.

"Harry, this is Alexander Stone. He's Kevin's brother."

"You an actor, too?"

"No. I'm an attorney." Given the grunting sound the fellow made, Alex assumed Harry wasn't exactly impressed by that news.

"I suppose it's better than nothing and steadier work than this acting stuff." He picked up Alex's cup and plate, then shifted his attention to Desiree. "What about you, girl? You going to eat the rest of that biscuit or you going to play with it all morning?"

"Don't rush me, Harry. You know I like to take my time eating. It's not good for my digestion to eat too fast."

"Missy, if you ate much slower, you'd still be sitting here when it came time for me to serve dinner. Never saw a female who could turn a ten-minute breakfast into a two-hour course."

He reached for her plate, and she grabbed the remaining half of her biscuit. "That's only because you're such a wonderful chef," she told his retreating back.

Alex watched as the other man deposited their dishes next to the sink and walked out of the kitchen. "He doesn't exactly fit the profile of what you'd call the friendly chef, does he?"

"Harry? He's a pussycat." She proceeded to spread a glob of strawberry jelly onto the piece of biscuit.

"Yeah? Then he's the first pussycat I've ever seen who has fists the size of hams and the word *Mother* tattooed across his biceps."

Desiree grinned. "That's because he used to be a cook

in the Navy before he retired two years ago. It's just him and his wife at home now. He misses cooking for those big groups of guys like he did on the ships.''

"Maybe he should have tried one of the burger places, then.''

"He did. He tried most of the fast-food chains and absolutely hated it. And as you pointed out, Harry doesn't exactly fit the profile of the celebrity chef that most of the better restaurants want these days, so that leaves him out. But he's a terrific cook. He'd had a really rough time finding the right place to hire him.''

"So you gave him a job.''

"I didn't *give* him anything. I needed a chef and was lucky enough to find Harry. He's a good chef. You said so yourself.'' She put down her knife. "Want a bite?''

"No, thanks.''

She bit into the flaky biscuit and sighed. The woman even made eating a sensual event, Alex decided as he watched her polish off the last of the biscuit.

"You've got a bit of jelly at the corner of your mouth,'' he told her.

But instead of using a napkin as he'd expected her to do, she tried licking at the spot with her tongue. Alex's stomach tightened as that pink tongue of hers flicked across her lips. "Did I get it?''

"No.''

Out came her tongue again and Alex felt the heat slap through him once more. Couldn't the woman use her napkin like a normal person? Or was she deliberately trying to drive him crazy? "Oh, for Pete's sake. Be still,'' he told her, coming to his feet. He came around the table, caught her chin in his hand, intending to wipe away the smear of strawberry jam with his napkin. But then she tipped her face up to him, stared at him with those sea green eyes. Desire whipped through him like a match to dry timber, setting off a raging fire inside him and shutting down his ability to reason. He lowered his mouth to hers.

Just a taste, he promised himself as he ran his tongue along the seam of her mouth. But then she parted her lips and what little control he'd had left snapped. He took the mouth she offered him, devoured it, as he sought and mated with her tongue. Still, it wasn't enough. He wanted—no, he needed more.

He drove his hands in her hair, pulling it free from the ribbon, and tangled his fists in the fiery silk as he'd wanted to do earlier. He drew her to her feet.

Desiree clutched at him, dug her fingers into his shoulders and allowed him to deepen the kiss. She tasted wonderful and forbidden. She tasted like innocence and sin. But tasting her, kissing her wasn't enough. He lifted his head, pulled her closer to him and groaned as she fitted herself against the ache in his lower body. Angling his head, he claimed her mouth again. He kissed her savagely, needing more of her fire, needing more of her heat. He spread his fingers along her hips, cupped her bottom and pressed her more tightly to him.

"Alex," she gasped, and the sound of his name on her lips set off another wave of heat through him.

"I want you," he whispered, his voice hoarse and gravelly with need. "Here. Now. I want you." On the table. On the floor. He didn't care where, just so long as he could sate this fire for her that raged in his blood.

"Yes," she murmured and sent the heat skyrocketing through him as she bit his lower lip.

It was all the encouragement he needed. Hands trembling, Alex pressed her against the table. This was madness, he told himself as he took her mouth again. But when she met the eager thrust of his tongue, he no longer cared. He smoothed his hands over the curve of her hips, squeezed the firm flesh, then sought the button of her shorts.

"Stop!"

Too lost in the feel of Desiree and the feel of her teeth nipping his ear, he barely registered the man's voice as he reached for the button of her shorts.

His fingers stilled at the sound of glass breaking, followed by a string of angry curses. Then suddenly the kitchen doors flew open.

"Stop this instant, you thief, or I'll cut your mangy heart out!"

Alex froze at the harsh command and jerked around just in time to see Harry come charging through the door into the kitchen with a knife in his hand.

Five

Desiree nearly stumbled as Alex jerked away from her, leaving her arms empty, her body throbbing. Still caught in the daze of Alex's lovemaking, she tried to steady her breathing. She managed to open her eyes just in time to see Harry rush past her with a knife in his hand in hot pursuit of two cats. Her cats!

"Stanley!" Desiree cried out as the black-and-white tom zipped by her with a trout clutched in his jaws. Blanche, the white female stray she'd picked up only last week, whizzed by after him.

"Come back here with that fish you sorry excuse for a cat! That's my lunch!"

The trio made a circle around the kitchen and ran past her again before Blanche shot to the right, out the opened screen door and into the yard. Stanley, with the trout still firmly clenched in his teeth, sped out the door behind her. Moving at a decidedly slower pace and cursing both cats as he went, Harry stormed out of the kitchen after them.

"Don't you think you should go after him?"

Desiree shook her head. "Those two are too fast for Harry. He'll never be able to catch them." Which was a good thing, Desiree admitted, because given the jellied feeling in her legs at the moment, she doubted that she'd be able to rescue her pets or Harry.

Mercy! Who'd have thought Alexander Stone would turn out to be such a champion kisser? Not that she'd had all that much experience with kissing—championship or otherwise, she admitted. She probably should have realized as much from their earlier, decidedly briefer encounter. Straightening her clothes, she combed a hand through her hair. And had it not been for Harry and her cats, she doubted seriously if they would have stopped at just kissing.

Desiree flushed, shocked by that realization. Great, Desiree, she chided herself silently. The man was already convinced she was some kind of vamp with designs on his brother. No telling what he'd think of her now. What in heaven's name had possessed her to let him kiss her that way? And the way she had kissed him back.

"He had a knife," Alex pointed out in a voice that held no hint of the turmoil she was experiencing over their kiss.

Stealing a glance at him, she frowned. In fact, he didn't look at all like a man who'd just told her he wanted her and had kissed her like a man possessed, like a man who couldn't get enough of her. Her frown deepened. Had she been wrong? Had *she* been the only one who'd been blown away by that kiss?

"Desiree, did you hear me? The man had a knife."

"I know," she replied, her mind still on that kiss. "But

Harry would never hurt Blanche or Stanley. I told you, he's a pussycat.''

"If you say so."

Desiree noted the distance Alex had put between them, and the way he was avoiding looking at her. Maybe Mr. Alexander Stone wasn't quite as unaffected as she'd thought. "It's nice of you to be concerned about Stanley and Blanche, though. I know you don't really like cats."

"I don't dislike cats. I'm allergic to them."

"I know, but still it was nice of you to be concerned." She took a step toward him.

He immediately stepped back. "I guess I'd better be going."

"Wouldn't you like some more coffee?"

"No, thanks. I need to get back to the cottage. I'm expecting a delivery from my office."

The rat. He was going to pretend that the kiss had never happened. Irked that he could so easily dismiss what had passed between them, she sauntered over to him. "Haven't you forgotten something?" she asked, deliberately lowering her voice to a husky whisper.

He narrowed his eyes, and she could feel the heat of his gaze like a touch as he ran it down the length of her and back up again. "I don't think so."

"No? Are you sure?" she asked, her pulse scattering as the air charged between them. She was crazy to push him, should be glad that things had stopped when they did. She moved a step closer to him instead. "I thought you said you needed to use the phone."

Fire snapped in his eyes for a moment, then it was quickly banked. He took a step back. "It can wait. I'm having my own line installed today. Thanks again for breakfast. I'll let you get back to work. But if you should hear from Kevin, I'd appreciate it if you'd let me know. I really do need to speak to him."

Fine, Desiree told herself as she watched Alex walk away. Maybe the man was a great kisser, but she'd be darned if she'd let a few kisses from him drive her crazy.

But he *was* driving her crazy, Desiree decided the next afternoon as Alex wandered into the theater during rehearsal and took a seat at one of the tables. Immersing herself in her role, she did her best to ignore him and completed the scene. "OK, everyone. That was pretty good. Let's break for five minutes and then we'll try that last scene."

As the cast dispersed, Alex rose and walked over to join her. "You're very good," he told her.

"You sound as though you're surprised," she countered.

"I guess I am."

"Why? Because you thought anyone who could really act wouldn't be caught dead doing dinner theater? That they'd be on Broadway or the London stage?"

"Tell me. Do you always respond to a compliment by pointing out your admirer's ignorance?"

Embarrassed, she felt the heat steal up her cheeks. "I'm sorry. I guess it's instinct, defending my decision to perform in dinner theaters instead of on the stage. But I still shouldn't have come at you like that."

"No, you shouldn't have. But then, I don't suppose I've exactly given you much reason to do otherwise."

He hadn't. He certainly hadn't done a thing for her peace of mind with his kisses. "Can we start again?"

"Sure. You were very good out there just now," he said, going along with her request.

"Thanks. I'm glad you enjoyed the performance."

"You're welcome."

Desiree laughed at the absurdity of the exchange. "Glad we got that out of the way. But I'm sure watching me rehearse wasn't the reason you came over." Given the flurry of activity she'd seen going on at the cottage with telephone installers and delivery men coming and going for the past two days, she was surprised he'd even bothered to leave the cottage at all.

"Actually, I was wondering if you'd heard anything from Kevin."

She should have known, Desiree told herself. Still, she couldn't shake the disappointment. "No. Not since before you arrived." At Alex's frown, she asked, "Is something wrong? You look worried. Or maybe I should say more worried than usual whenever Kevin's name comes up."

"Actually, I am worried. At least a little. The detective I hired to find Kevin hasn't been able to locate him. Evidently, he's not using any of his credit cards or writing any personal checks."

"You hired a detective to find him?"

"Of course. You didn't expect me to just hang around here and wait for him to show up, did you?"

Actually, that had been exactly what she'd expected him to do. "I guess I hadn't thought about it much one way or the other. What *did* you find out?" she asked curiously.

"You mean besides the fact that Kevin isn't living here with you as I'd initially suspected and that the two of you aren't engaged?"

Shock quickly turned to irritation. "Since you haven't spoken to Kevin and obviously didn't believe me, just how did you manage to come to those conclusions?"

"I had the detective ask around, speak to some of Kevin's friends and yours. There's no question that Kevin's infatuated with you and that you're rather fond of him, but the general consensus is that the two of you aren't lovers."

Desiree nearly choked with outrage. "You mean to tell me that you actually questioned my friends?"

"Not me, actually. But my detective—"

"How dare you!" She glared at him, curled her hands into tight fists. "You had no right to investigate me, to question my friends."

Alex caught her fists in his hand. His eyes hard, his voice even harder, he told her, "I had every right. Especially considering what's happening between us."

"Nothing's happening between us."

"Not yet."

"Not ever," she told him, and jerked her hands free.

"I, for one, hope you're right. The last thing I need is to become involved with you. Besides the fact that my kid brother may or may not think he's in love with you, an actress in some backwater Louisiana town doesn't fit into my plans now or in the future."

"Well, that's just dandy, because you don't exactly fit my description of Prince Charming, either."

"That's good, because I have no intention of playing Prince Charming for you or anyone else. I've never believed in fairy tales and I'm not about to start now."

"Since I don't recall asking you to audition for the role, I guess you have nothing to worry about." But for some reason, his remark about not believing in fairy tales made her stomach sink.

"That's where you're wrong. Because despite the fact that I find you unsuitable as a lover, nothing seems to change the fact that I want you. Judging from your response when I kissed you, I suspect you feel the same way. Which presents us with a problem. The longer I'm forced to hang around here waiting for Kevin, the harder it's going to be for me not to do something about it."

Desiree felt as though she'd been both kissed and slapped at the same time. She felt warmed by the knowledge that he wanted her and insulted that he hated the fact that he did. "Then I'll make it easy for you, Alex, by assuring you that *nothing* is going to happen between us because *I* don't want anything to happen between us. Now, why don't you pack up that ego of yours and head home to Boston. When Kevin gets back, I'll tell him to give you a call."

Turning on her heel, she walked away from him feigning a calmness she was far from feeling. She clapped her hands for the cast. "OK, everyone. Back to work."

Instead of leaving as she had hoped, Alex leaned against one of the posts to the far right of the stage and watched. Reminding herself that she was an actress, Desiree tried her best to shut his image from her thoughts and blocked out the next scene of the play. Satisfied everyone was in place, she turned to Harry who had agreed to substitute for Kevin's part in the rehearsal. "All right, Harry. Do you understand where you're supposed to come in?"

"Yeah. I understand, but I still don't like it. I'm no actor. I'm a cook."

"I know. But until Kevin gets back, I don't have anyone else. Please just do me a favor and read the lines, anyway?"

Harry mumbled something, which Desiree decided to take as a yes. With a nod of her head, she gave the signal for them to begin. They ran through the scene just as they'd rehearsed, and after the minister delivered his lines, giving Harry his cue, Desiree waited. And waited.

Sighing, she turned to Harry. "Harry," she prompted. In his stained apron, with his tattooed biceps and bald head, Harry didn't come close to resembling the man her character was supposedly in love with. "Harry," she called again.

Harry stepped forward stiffly and proceeded to deliver the wrong line.

"No, Harry," Desiree corrected. "That's my line. You're supposed to read the part above that one." After pointing out to him the portion of the script that he was supposed to read, she returned to her previous position.

Once more they ran through the scene. And once more Harry flubbed the lines. "That's it. I quit."

"Harry!"

"I'm sorry, Desiree. But I'm no actor. I feel like an idiot saying this stuff. You're just going to have to get yourself somebody else to read that stuff or wait until Kevin gets back."

"There *isn't* anyone else. Please, Harry, just try it one more time. For me."

"No use batting them eyes at me, girl. I ain't gonna do it," he told her, crossing his beefy arms. "Why don't you ask him?" He jerked his head in Alex's direction.

"No," Desiree replied immediately. The last thing she wanted was to have Alex acting the role of her lover even if it was just for the play.

"Why not? It's Kevin's part and he's Kevin's brother. Besides, from what I heard, he did a pretty good job of it the other day."

"Forget it. Peter, you can read Kevin's lines." She took the script pages from Harry and shoved them into the other man's hands.

"But I'm the best man. And I'm supposed to get this guy to leave the church. How am I going to do that if it's myself I'm trying to haul out?"

"I don't know. We'll work it out somehow. Just read Kevin's lines for now. OK?"

"That won't be necessary." Alex pushed away from the post he'd been leaning against and walked over to where they were standing. "If you're just looking for someone to read the lines. I'll do it."

Desiree hesitated. But Peter was already shoving the pages into Alex's hands.

"All right," she agreed, too frazzled to argue further.

"So, what's the situation?" he asked. "I want to be sure I've got the setup clear in my mind."

"You don't need to worry about having the setup clear in your mind. All you're going to do is read the lines."

"But he's right, Des. If he's into the role, it will make it that much easier for the rest of us to rehearse," Charlie, the minister, explained.

Deciding the best thing to do was to get this over with, Desiree outlined the gist of the scene. "It's the last scene of the play. I'm the only woman you've ever loved, but your stubborn pride has kept us apart. Now that I'm about to marry another man, your brother, you realize your mistake and come to stop the wedding. Got it?"

"Got it."

She had to give him credit, Desiree admitted a short time later. He nailed the scene and was nearly as convincing as he'd been that first day she'd met him. Throwing herself into her role, she marched over to Alex. "Give me one reason why I should listen to anything you have to say?"

Alex snagged her by the waist, pulled her into his arms just as the script dictated. "Because I love you," he said, his eyes darkening with desire. "And if you're honest with yourself, you'll admit that you love me."

Desiree's heart pounded as she stared into his eyes. She touched his cheek, but the answering heat in her had nothing to do with the script.

"Admit it," he whispered, his mouth now only a breath away from her own. "Admit that it's me you love, Desiree. Me. Not my brother."

A groan went up from somewhere behind her. "Her name's supposed to be Kate," Charlie corrected.

Charlie's voice snapped the seductive spell she'd fallen under, and she pushed at Alex's shoulders. "He's right. The character's name is Kate," she corrected.

From the dazed expression on his face, she suspected that Alex had been just as caught up in the role-playing as she had. He reached down and retrieved the script pages that had fallen to the floor. "Right. Kate," he repeated.

"Other than the mess-up with the name, I'd say the two of you were pretty good together," Charlie, the minister, informed them. "Must run in the family. If Kevin doesn't make it back in time for the opening, maybe Alex here could take over his role."

"Kevin will be back," Desiree assured him. He'd better, she told herself silently. Because she wasn't sure how much longer she'd be able to keep her sanity with Alex around.

"All right. All that's left is the kiss and the switch at the altar. Des, you two want to take it from the top and run through the scene again?"

"No."

"Yes."

Charlie's gaze swung from one to the other. "Well, which is it?"

"No," Desiree said firmly. "There's no need to rehearse the kiss."

"Ah, but I disagree. We wouldn't want your timing to be off, now, would we?" And before she realized his intent, Alex was beside her, sliding his arm around her waist and bending her back over his arm.

"Stop—" She started to protest only to have the word cut off by his mouth. And then she was lost in the feel of his mouth claiming her own, the demanding thrust of his tongue. When he finally lifted his head, Desiree did something she'd never done before in her life. She completely forgot the rest of her lines.

"I don't care how many strings you have to pull. It's been more than a week, and except for that message he left on my answering machine in Boston, no one's heard a word from Kevin. I want him found."

As the detective ran through a litany of measures he'd taken to locate his brother, Alex flicked back the curtain at the window of his cottage and spotted Desiree walking on the pathway leading to the gazebo. The morning sunlight caught her hair, turning it to fire, as she came more clearly into view. She tipped her head back in laughter at the puppy running circles around her feet. She leaned over; the denim cutoffs she wore stretched across her hips, hiking up to the tops of those long legs as she picked up a stick and tossed it for the pup. Then she turned, and Alex's mouth went dry at the sight of her back—naked, save for the knotted ends of her halter top. The puppy came racing back to her with the stick, ears flapping and legs tangling, before it tumbled clumsily at her feet. He knew just how the puppy felt, Alex thought as he released the curtain and swung away from the window. His feet had felt anything but steady since the first time he'd laid eyes on her.

And it simply had to stop. He rubbed at his eyes with his free hand, trying to wipe Desiree's image from his mind. The woman had him in a constant state of confusion. He couldn't think. He could barely function for wanting her.

"Alex? Alex, are you still there?"

He'd missed half of what the detective had said to him, Alex realized. Something else that was totally out of character for him. "Sorry. What was that again?"

"I said if the phone bill and bank statements don't give us anything more to go on, I can report Kevin's credit cards stolen, shut off his cell phone. Cutting off his source of cash might force him out into the open. Sooner or later he'll need to use his cards or try to replenish his cash. How far do you want me to go with this?"

"As far as you have to. Do whatever it takes, Fletcher, but find my brother."

"Whatever you say. You're the boss."

Only he didn't feel much like the boss. He certainly didn't feel like a man who was calling the shots at the moment. He didn't feel in control at all. After giving the detective final instructions, Alex punched the Off button and put down the telephone. Returning to the desk he'd set up in the center of the room, he sat down in the chair.

For a man who held three degrees and had been touted by the business community as a brilliant strategist, he wasn't doing too well. He still hadn't located Kevin, let alone nixed his plans to drop out of law school or put a stop to any notions his brother may or may not have about marrying Desiree. He'd leased a cottage for a year in a place he didn't want to be. And the only person who seemed to be falling for his aborted scheme to thwart Desiree's romance with his brother by offering himself as a target was him. While she had responded to his kisses, *he* had been the one left hungry and aching for more. Guilt washed over him. Not once when he'd held her in his arms or had tasted her with his mouth had he been thinking of his brother.

Disgusted with himself, Alex picked up the folder containing the report the detective agency had compiled for him on Desiree. He'd already read the thing twice and, given his photographic memory, he could recite every detail in it verbatim. He opened the folder, anyway. A smiling Desiree stared back at him from a photograph, and he noted again how the camera had somehow managed to capture that spark of excitement in her eyes. Skimming over the chart of vital statistics, he noted even her bra size—34C—had been included in the report. Desire stirred inside him as he recalled just how close he'd come to verifying the accuracy of that figure for himself.

Disturbed by his reaction, Alex flicked to the next page of the report. She didn't lack for friends, male or female. And though the consensus had been that she and Kevin weren't lovers, a point which she had insisted was true, she didn't deny that she and Kevin were close. Wondering just how close the two of them were had been one of the things that had made him steer clear of her for the past few days. That and the fact that his usually analytical mind didn't seem to operate on all cylinders whenever he was anywhere near her.

Scanning the financial data again, he shook his head. The woman had an acting career that moved in spurts and trickles at best. It was impossible to view her work history and not think of his own mother's determined leap from Las Vegas dancer to millionaire's wife and then rich divorcee. Grimacing at the unpleasant memory, Alex noted her pitiful bank balance and the small fortune she owed the bank on Magnolia House. Given her lack of experience, she'd need a miracle to make the place pay off. Or someone like his brother with a multimillion-dollar trust fund to fall back on. On paper she fit the profile of a woman in need of a rich husband.

Yet the woman he'd discovered seemed to be a soft touch for every person or creature that crossed her path. Who but a hopeless romantic would ever name their pets after characters from Tennessee Williams plays? That certainly didn't fit with his image of a mercenary female with designs on his brother's trust fund. Even her brushes with the law—disturbing the peace by chaining herself to a tree to save an old, diseased oak slated for destruction, and theft for refusing to return a costume in a dispute over wages owed her by a theater operator—painted the picture of a bleeding heart, not a scheming gold digger. So which one was she?

Alex was no closer to an answer when the sound of a crash in the kitchen had him shoving the report aside to investigate. Maggie stood on the countertop, licking at the remnants of dried milk on his coffee cup. "How did you get in here?" he asked the little black cat.

At her meow, Alex walked over and stroked her silky head. He spied the tear in the screen and the open window. "So that's how you got in," he told her as he shut the window and made a mental note to replace the screen.

The kitten went back to working at the hardened milk on the rim of the cup. "Don't tell me your mistress got you stuck on that milk and coffee thing, too."

The cat looked up at him and gave him another meow as though in answer to his question, then she flicked her little sandpapery tongue across his fingers.

"Good thing I've been taking my antihistamines," he told her, feeling the slight stinging begin in his eyes. Despite the minor discomfort, he gave her another scratch behind her ears. "How about some milk?" Reaching for a saucer, he filled it with milk and set it in front of Maggie. He watched her drink for a few minutes, then gave her another scratch behind the ear. "I'm going back to work," he told her. "Let me know when you're finished and I'll let you out."

But several hours later, Maggie was still there, curled up in his lap while he worked. Alex stroked her with one hand while he flicked on his recorder to dictate another change in the contracts he'd been reviewing. "On page twenty-three, section C, have the language amended to reflect the changes I've marked on the page." He flipped to the next page. "And on page twenty-four—"

"Alex?"

Alex glanced up to see Desiree standing in the open doorway holding a tray with a pitcher and a plate of cookies. Sometime during the afternoon, he'd opened the door and windows following a cooling summer rainstorm. She'd changed the cutoffs and halter top he'd spied her in earlier for a white, flowing skirt and peasant-style blouse that showed off her smooth shoulders. Alex wondered if he'd be able to see that heart-shaped mole if she turned around.

"The door was open," she explained. "Mind giving me a hand with this?"

"Sorry," he said, shooting to his feet and upsetting Maggie in the process. "Let me get that for you." He took the tray from her.

"Maggie, I'd wondered where you'd gone off to."

"She showed up here a few hours ago," Alex explained as he pushed aside a stack of papers and made room for the tray on his desk. "I, umm, I gave her a can of tuna fish," he admitted.

"Uh-oh. I'm afraid you've *really* done it then. Her heart's probably yours forever—which means, she'll be back."

Alex shrugged. "It's all right." He'd never had a pet, growing up, in part because of his allergies and in part because a lot of his youth had been spent in military boarding school. So it was sort of nice having one around for a while.

"What about your allergies?" she asked, eyeing him closely as she evidently searched for signs of the weeping and sneezing he'd exhibited the last time the cat had been in his presence.

"I got a prescription for some antihistamine tablets.

My eyes still sting a bit, but it's not quite as bad." As though she found the humans' discussion boring, Maggie trotted out the open door and into the fading sunlight.

Silence hung between them for long moments. Finally Desiree said, "I brought you some lemonade and a plate of Harry's peanut butter cookies."

Alex waited, unsure what to make of her unexpected visit or her offer. He'd suspected she'd been avoiding him for the past few days, but for the life of him hadn't quite figured out why. He took the glass she handed him and sniffed. "Should I have it tested for hemlock first?"

"I knew this was a stupid idea. Forget it."

She started to turn when he caught her arm. "Hang on a minute. I was only teasing. What's a stupid idea?"

Instead of answering him, she snitched a cookie from the tray and began to nibble on it. "They said I should come talk to you first."

"They?"

"Harry and the rest of the gang," she explained. "Harry thought the cookies might help me to make peace with you."

"I didn't realize we were at war."

Glaring at him, she held out the plate of cookies. Nerves, Alex decided as he took a cookie he didn't want and began to eat it. He hadn't thought anything could make Desiree nervous. Yet, judging from the way she attacked the cookie with precise, little bites and then grabbed another, he'd lay odds the lady was nervous now, because one of the many things he'd observed about her was that she snacked when she was nervous. Alex reached for another cookie himself and bit into the peanut butter crisp. "Harry was right. The cookies are a great peace offering. Now you want to tell me what this is all about?"

"Kevin called."

Alex froze with the cookie halfway to his mouth. "When?"

"A few hours ago."

"And you're just now coming to tell me about it? Did you tell him I was here? That I wanted to speak to him?"

"Yes," Desiree replied tightly. "He's promised to call you back tomorrow."

"Where is he?" Alex demanded.

"I don't know."

"Don't give me that. You know where he is. You've probably known all along."

"No, I don't. I mean, he's not staying in any one place at the moment. He promised he'd call you tomorrow and explain everything."

"Explain what?" Alex asked, an uneasy sensation prickling at the base of his neck. "What is it you aren't telling me?"

When she didn't respond, he caught her by the arms and forced her to look at him. "Tell me. What is it that Kevin needs to explain to me?"

"That he's decided to get married."

Six

"You're not going to marry him," Alex declared.

"But I—"

"But what? You love him? You expect me to believe that after the way you came apart in my arms?" He moved in on her, caging her between the desk and himself.

Desiree's pulse skittered at the fierce emotion emanating from him, at the desire burning hot and dark in those black eyes. Try as she might, she was unable to stop herself from responding to him. "Alex, you don't understand. If you'd just let me explain, Kevin and I—"

"I won't let you marry him."

And before she could say another word, before she could tell him that it wasn't her that Kevin wanted to marry, he took possession of her mouth. Her mind. Her heart. There was nothing nice or tame or polite about his kiss. It wasn't the kiss of a stuffed-shirt businessman whose life revolved around bottom lines and financial statements. It wasn't the kiss of a genius who held a string of degrees and equated love to a chemical reaction that could be monitored and controlled. It was the kiss of a ruthless warrior, a man who seized what he wanted. A man who would make love to a woman hard and fast, hot and thorough. A man who would demand everything from his partner and give everything of himself in return.

Alex tore his mouth from hers, and Desiree thought she would collapse from that mind-shattering kiss. His breaths came ragged and fast. So did hers. She leaned against him, not sure she could stand on her own. "I'm not going to marry Kevin," she whispered, her breath still shaky, her heart even shakier.

Triumph gleamed in his eyes, making him look every inch the warrior he reminded her of. He swiped an arm across the desk, sending folders and papers flying to the floor.

"Alex!" Her pulse jumped as he reached for her. Catching her by the waist, he lifted her up onto the desk and moved between her legs. Her blood began to spin as he curled his fingers around her ankles. And then those fingers started to move. His hands were hard and warm as he ran them up along her calves, over her thighs, pushing the hem of her skirt up until it puddled around her hips.

The fax machine hummed on the table just a few feet away, rattling the tray with the pitcher of lemonade and cookies sitting beside it. Somewhere a dog barked, a door slammed. Desiree barely heard any of it above the frantic beating of her heart and the roar of desire in her blood.

She could feel the threads of control slipping fast. But first she needed to tell him, make sure he understood that there was never anything between her and Kevin, that it wasn't her that Kevin was planning to marry. "Alex, I need—"

Her breath hitched as his fingers stroked her through her panties. All thoughts tumbled from her head. Closing her eyes, Desiree held on to him, trembled as he continued the rhythmic stroking with his fingers while his mouth, that oh-so-clever mouth of his, created havoc with her throat.

Surrendering to the dizzying heat and feel of his touch, she clutched at his shoulders. The first wave of pleasure slammed into her and nearly stole her breath away. Shuddering, she nearly wept as Alex continued to touch her, to pleasure her with his mouth and his hands, and sent her spiraling over peak after peak. Just when she was sure she'd faint with the sheer joy of his touch, Alex withdrew his hand. Then his mouth abandoned that sensitive spot at her ear. Weak, her body still sensitized, Desiree swayed. "Alex, I can't believe... I didn't know—"

She sucked in a breath, curled her hands into fists as she felt his mouth on her, his tongue, wet and hot, stroking her through the silk of her panties.

It was erotic and decadent.

It was wonderful and wicked.

It wasn't enough.

She wanted more. She wanted him.

Thanks to Kevin's stories of how Alex had always been there for him, she had admired Alex, been half in love with him before she'd ever set eyes on him. Meeting the man with the dark angel's face and practical heart who believed there was no such thing as magic in the world, no such thing as love, should have nipped those tender feelings for him in the bud.

It hadn't. She'd told herself that the two of them were like fire and ice—polar opposites in lifestyles, in goals, in beliefs. But that hadn't stopped her feelings for him from growing. None of it had mattered a lick. Probably because while the man thought he had a heart of granite, she had known better. He was as much of a marshmallow as she was. He'd taken in his younger brother and would dance through fire to protect him, she was sure. He'd even been too much of a softie to turn Maggie away—despite the fact that her presence made him physically ill.

She didn't need another stray in her life—especially not one who set her body on fire with needs she hadn't known she had. But she couldn't walk away from him. There was a loneliness beneath his bravado, a raw hunger when he looked at her, a need that she tasted in his kiss. It tugged at her heart as nothing else could.

"Desiree." Her name was a desperate plea on his lips as he lifted his head and pushed himself to his feet. "Look at me," he commanded.

She opened her eyes and stared at his face. His eyes were as wild as a summer storm, as dark as a midnight sky. She reached out and touched his face. He caught her fingers, took them into his mouth, grazed them with his teeth.

She didn't stand a chance. Her heart went plunging off that cliff. She was in love with Alexander Stone. This complex, maddening man had stolen her heart like the cleverest of thieves, and she didn't have a prayer of getting it back.

She'd never been a woman to play it safe, Desiree admitted. Her life, her profession, even Magnolia House had been one risk after another. She wasn't going to play it safe now, she decided, and brought her mouth to his.

Alex made an animal cry deep in his throat that sent the blood pumping fast and furiously through her veins. And then he was devouring her mouth with his. She could taste herself on him as his tongue dove in, dipping deeper and deeper still. He cupped her bottom, squeezed her with his fingers, then pressed her against him.

He was aroused, rock hard and heavy. She could feel his belt buckle digging in at her waist, feel the teeth of his metal zipper brushing against her inner thigh. Desire, already wound tight in her belly, grew tighter still.

"Alex," she gasped as he tore away the silk of her panties and spread her thighs apart.

"I want you," he told her.

Heart pounding with the speed of a jet, Desiree heard the fax line ring again, heard the vibration of the table. Or maybe it was her pulse vibrating, she thought dizzily as she reached for him.

The tray with the lemonade and cookies went crashing to the floor. And Alex jerked away from her as though he'd been shot.

Desiree froze. It seemed an eternity before she could breathe again. Shoving down her skirt, she finally looked over at Alex. He was slumped in a chair, his hand covering his face. His shoulders rose and fell as he drew in deep breaths. Her legs still shaky, Desiree eased the tips of her toes to the floor, needing the feel of solid ground beneath her feet. Finally, she said, "Alex?"

He scrubbed his hand down his face. He looked dazed, shell-shocked. Guilty. "Damn! I don't know what I was thinking of. I never meant for that to happen."

"It's all right."

He shoved a hand through his hair. "I'm sorry. I just don't know what in the hell came over me. I never meant for things to get so out of hand."

He glanced over to the floor where he'd tossed her torn panties. From the look on his face, he obviously was having some big-time regrets, Desiree realized. "Alex, it really is all right."

"No, it isn't." He stood, shoved his hands into his pockets and started to pace. After several quick trips in front of the desk, he swung around to face her. "Do you want to press charges?"

Desiree blinked. "Press charges?"

"Yeah. For me—for me jumping you the way I did."

Desiree sighed. Evidently the man had no idea of just how much of a participant she had been. "I hate to disappoint you when you're so intent on beating yourself up, but you didn't 'jump' me."

"What do you call that then?" he demanded, pointing to the wad of white silk on the floor. He shoved his hands through his hair again, then jammed them into his pants' pockets. "For God's sake, I tore your panties off you."

"Yes, you did," she said smiling. "That was a first for me. And I have to tell you it was quite gratifying to know I could inspire that type of passion in you." But despite her joking, there was no erasing that frown from his face. So she reached up with both hands and stroked his whisker-rough jaws. "Personally, I found it terribly exciting. Erotic. I've never had someone make love to me on a desk before. Well, I guess we didn't really make love, did we? But you know what I mean."

He stared at her as though she'd lost her mind. Perhaps she had, Desiree admitted. But there was something awfully flattering to her, as a woman, to know that kissing her could rattle the oh-so-proper and in-control Alexander Stone. Especially when the man knocked her socks off without even trying.

"And in case you hadn't noticed, I was very much a willing participant."

Judging from the way his brows had scrunched up, that comment seemed only to confuse him more. Unable to resist, she smoothed her fingers across his beautiful mouth, then followed through with her lips.

* * *

It wasn't the first time she'd kissed him. Hell, they'd done a hell of a lot more than just kiss a few minutes ago, and as she'd just pointed out, she had been a willing participant in that out-of-control, melt-his-teeth-fillings kiss.

And it wasn't going to happen again. He'd made that decision not two minutes ago, because he knew kissing Desiree Mason again, regardless of how willing she might be, would be a mistake.

But he hadn't counted on her touching his cheeks with those oh-so-soft hands. And he certainly hadn't counted on her rubbing those cookie-sweetened lips of hers against his. Or her sneaking her arms up around his neck and easing her body closer to his. No way was he going to kiss her. He positively wouldn't dip his tongue between her parted lips for another taste.

He had no intention whatsoever of doing either of those things, but he did. And now that he had touched her lips, dipped inside for another taste, he didn't seem to be able to stop.

He kissed her—long and slow and deep. Lifting his head, he angled his mouth and went in for another taste. When she finally ended the kiss, he was rock hard and aching once more and wondering what had happened to his resolve not to kiss her again.

"Wow." She slumped against him. "I don't know what all your fancy degrees are in, but if you don't have one in kissing, you should. You're a great kisser, Alexander Stone."

He was a great kisser? He doubted he had a single filling left in his mouth. Surely they had melted with all that heat.

"Tell me, are all genius businessmen such great kissers?"

Alex frowned at the question. "I don't know. I'm not sure any tests have ever been conducted on it."

She tipped her head back to look at him, then a smile spread across her lips. "I was kidding, Alex. Not about your being a great kisser. You are. But about wanting to know if all geniuses kissed as well as you do."

"I knew that," he fibbed, feeling foolish for taking her so literally. But he couldn't prevent that jolt of pleasure that her words had brought him.

"And as much as I'd enjoy kissing you some more, I don't think it's such a good idea. At least not until we've cleared up a few things."

She was right, and he agreed with her one hundred percent. They did need to clear up some things between them. So why in the world did that thought disappoint him? And why did he have such a sinking feeling that he wasn't going to like what she had to say?

"We also need to talk about Kevin. I promised him I'd speak with you before he calls."

Guilt shot through him with the swiftness and sureness of a bullet fired by an expert marksman.

Kevin.

How in the hell had he let himself forget Kevin? His brother was the reason he'd come here in the first place. Protecting Kevin had been the reason he'd come up with the cockamamie notion to try to lure Desiree's attentions to him. The first time he'd kissed her, he had told himself he'd done it for Kevin's sake. The second time he'd kissed her, he'd sworn it was for Kevin. No way in hell had his almost making love to her tonight been on behalf of his brother.

His brother hadn't even entered his thoughts—except when she'd said Kevin was getting married. Then he'd wanted to murder his brother, because there was no way he could allow him to marry Desiree. "You said he was getting married."

"Yes, that's what he says, and before we go any further, I'm not the bride."

"Then who is she?"

She avoided his eyes. "Listen, why don't I help you clean up this mess first and then we'll talk."

At her mention of the mess, Alex remembered the reason he wasn't at this very minute lying naked with Desiree across the top of the desk. Were it not for the wobbly table holding the fax machine, he'd probably be buried deep inside of her right now.

He bit back a groan at that dangerous image and tried to erase it from his mind. He shifted his attention to where the pitcher of lemonade lay on its side, chunks of ice floating in what was left of the drink. Peanut butter cookies lay in broken chunks amid pieces of what was once a plate. The tray leaned drunkenly against the leg of the table. Papers and contracts—contracts he'd spent hours reading, making notations to—lay scattered like leaves across the floor, sopping up whatever lemonade had missed the rug. The fax machine continued to hum noisily, spitting out more sheets of paper to join the chaos on the floor.

Desiree leaned over to pick up the pitcher, and Alex's pulse slam-dunked as her blouse dipped, giving him a glimpse of her breasts. Breasts that he knew would be warm and firm and just fill the palms of his hands.

Alex swore. Something else he seemed to be doing a lot more of lately, he realized and made a vow to stop. Turning away from her, he rubbed the knotted muscles at the base of his neck. What in the hell was wrong with him, anyway? He might lose his temper occasionally, but he never lost control—not like this—not emotionally, certainly not while having a sexual encounter with a woman. He'd always prided himself on his iron-tight control and firm grip on his emotions. Yet every time he got within ten feet of Desiree his control turned to dust.

He spied her torn panties on the floor and swiped them up in his fist. The material was soft and silky. His blood churned in his veins as he remembered the taste of her on his lips, the whiskey-low cries of pleasure she'd made when he'd touched her.

"Alex? Are you all right?"

"No." He wasn't all right. He hadn't been all right since the first time he'd set eyes on her. But that was going to change, he promised himself. Tossing the ruined panties in the trash can, he made a mental note to replace them for her. He was a smart man, he reminded himself. A certified genius for pity's sake. And only a fool would stick around and let himself get tangled in her seductive web.

He was no fool. As soon as he found out who it was Kevin was planning to marry and where his brother was hiding out, he was packing his bags and getting out of here and as far away from Desiree Mason as he could.

But by the time most of the damage had been cleared away, Alex was feeling only marginally in control. Now that he'd had a glimpse of what making love to Desiree would be like, he couldn't keep himself from looking at those long legs when she walked past him. Not when his body eagerly reminded him how soft and smooth those legs had felt under his hands.

And when she leaned over to pick up a stack of folders, his brain refused to let him forget that she wasn't wearing any panties underneath that skirt. And when she wiped up lemonade from the tabletop, his cursed photographic memory registered that the gleam of red gold hair caught in the lamplight was the exact shade that he'd glimpsed in a more secret, intimate part of her body.

There was no point in torturing himself this way, Alex decided. A relationship with Desiree Mason, even an affair, was out of the question. Even if Kevin were out of the picture, and he wasn't a hundred percent convinced that he was, to conduct an affair with the woman would be plain stupid. "I think we've got the worst of it," he told her, tossing the sponge into the bucket. He got up off his knees. "I'll see about having a cleaning service come out tomorrow to clean the carpet and the floor."

Alex stretched his back and glanced over at Desiree patiently laying out the wet pages of his reports one by one across the carpet and floor to dry. He'd be damned if his hormones—which apparently had gone wacko from the heat and humidity in this town—didn't find even the sight of her kneeling on the floor arousing.

"Look at all these papers," she said, gazing up at him out of those sea green eyes. "Do you have any idea how many trees are killed each year just to supply paper?"

He quoted her the figure. "I make sure all our offices recycle."

"I should have known you'd be conscientious with something like that."

He felt that jab to his gut again when she smiled up at him. Irritated that she could affect him so, he reached down for the bucket. "I'm going to put this stuff away. You can just leave the rest of those papers and files on the floor. I'll sort them out later."

After dispensing with the cleaning supplies and washing his hands, not to mention dunking his face and head under the cold water faucet, Alex could feel his control begin to return. He walked into the living room, determined to get this talk over with and send her on her way.

But instead of finding her seated on the couch or a chair as he'd hoped, she was still kneeling on the floor, her face paper white and her eyes filled with pain as she clutched an open file in her hands.

Alex knew at once that she'd found his report on her. She looked up at him. Guilt bolted through him like a runaway horse at her stricken expression. He walked over to her and held out his hand. "That's a confidential report."

"It's a report on *me*. You had me investigated." It was an accusation, not a question.

"Yes, I did."

Slowly she came to her feet. "There are things in here—private things—about me, about my family, about my friends. There's a list here of all the plays I've been in. The places I've worked. You even have the name of the first boy I fell in love with." She flipped through the pages, temper or embarrassment—he wasn't sure which—bringing color back into her cheeks.

"My bra size?"

Alex flushed. "The agency was very thorough."

"I'll say. They've even provided you with the name of the first man I slept with."

"Like I said, the agency was thorough."

"And these notes, these interviews with people about me and Kevin, about our friendship."

"I told you I had a detective checking into your relationship with my brother."

"I didn't believe you."

"You should have. I needed to know what type of hold you had on Kevin. Just how serious your relationship with him was." He'd hurt her. He could see it in her eyes, and it made him feel lower than the belly of a snake.

"And if it had been serious, what were you planning to do, Alex? Buy me off? Is that the reason you were making notes on my financial statement?" She held up the report in her fist. "Were you going to offer me money to get out of Kevin's life?"

Shame heated his neck and face. He had been prepared to do exactly that. "If I'd thought it would have worked, yes. I would have offered you money to get out of Kevin's life. But I knew inside of forty-eight hours that you weren't a woman who could be swayed by money."

"So you decided to see if you could seduce me instead."

And he'd abandoned that idea almost as quickly. He hadn't had a prayer of seducing her—not when he was the one being seduced.

Evidently his silence had given her the answer. "Well, I certainly hope Kevin appreciates just how much you were willing to do to save him from me." She handed him the folder and turned to leave.

"Desiree."

She paused at the door and looked back at him.

He told himself to stay where he was, to keep his distance. His traitorous legs refused to obey him. He was beside her in two strides. He tipped her chin up with his fingertip. "What happened between us tonight didn't have a thing to do with Kevin. I wanted you. I still want you." One look into those bruised eyes of hers and he could feel himself starting to sink. He dropped his hand and took a step back.

"But you don't want to want me."

"No, I don't."

"Why?" she asked.

"Because for you desire and sex would equate to love. It would lead to other expectations, to fairy-tale endings that don't have a prayer of coming true."

"Because you don't believe in love or fairy tales."

"No and I never will." He'd watched both of his parents search for the fairy-tale happily-ever-afters and make themselves and the seven spouses they'd subsequently married and divorced miserable when they never found it. He'd sworn a long time ago it wasn't going to happen to him.

"How very sad for you."

"Not sad, just realistic."

"And lonely." She sighed. "Considering that you're the one who raised Kevin, it's a miracle your jaded outlook on life never rubbed off on him. He actually wants to get married. I was supposed to try to soften you up a bit to the idea for him, but I think he'll have to do it himself when he calls you tomorrow."

For the life of him, he didn't understand how being with her could make him completely forget about his brother. "Where is Kevin?"

"He didn't say."

"But—"

"I'm not up to a grilling, Alex. Kevin said he'd call you in the morning. You'll just have to wait and get your answers from him."

"After I talk to him and straighten out this mess, I'll be leaving," he told her. He knew it was the best thing for both of them.

"And I suppose you want a refund on your lease."

"No. I'll honor the lease." Besides he knew she could use the money. "I'll drop the key off tomorrow before I leave."

Only, three days later Alex still hadn't dropped off the key to the cottage, and as far as she could determine he was still there.

He'd talked to Kevin. That much she knew. According to Harry, who'd been fishing from the bridge overlooking the lake by the cottage. He'd spied Alex feeding Brick, the new puppy she'd inherited, on the front porch the next morning when he'd evidently gotten the call from Kevin. At least she thought it must have been Kevin who'd called since Harry had reported hearing Alex let loose with a string of curses that had sent Brick running for cover.

So why was the confounded man still here? He'd made it all too clear that while he might want her, he didn't want to want her. Of course, that hadn't stopped her from wanting him. Or from thinking about him.

She'd tried anger at his having that report run on her. It hadn't even lasted until she'd gotten out of the cottage. She just was no good at holding a grudge—never had been—and especially not when she understood why he'd done it. How could she fault Alex for trying to protect his brother? Wouldn't she have done the same thing for her sisters? Besides, hadn't she interfered in her sister Lorelei's love life when she'd become convinced her sister was marrying the wrong man? No, try as she might, she wasn't angry with him. And for the first time in her life, losing herself in a role wasn't working.

"I'll get over him," she told herself. After all, Alex wasn't the first man she'd cared about and parted ways with. But he was the first one that had ever made her feel that she belonged in his arms. And he was the first man with whom she'd ever wanted to spend those happy-ever-afters. He was a man she was simply going to have to forget.

And the best way to get over him was a chocolate fix, Desiree decided and headed for the kitchen. "How about a snack?" she asked Maggie as the cat trotted behind her. She shook a handful of kitty treats from the box and placed them in front of Maggie. Then she rooted through the pantry until she found a container of Harry's chocolate chip, peanut butter cookies for herself. The perfect cure for a bruised heart. She counted out four of the calorie-laden creations. She could have four, she told herself and made a solemn vow to skip lunch the next day. Four of Harry's chocolate chip, peanut butter wonders and Alex Stone would be a distant memory.

She went back for a fifth cookie. By the time she'd finished it and had reached for a sixth, she was no closer to banishing Alex from her mind and heart than she had been three days ago.

"You keep eating those cookies, girl, and you're not going to be able to fit into that wedding dress costume of yours on opening night."

Desiree looked up and spotted Harry standing across the table, a worried expression on his face. "I was hungry," she explained.

"Hungry, my foot. You're brooding over that man again."

"I don't know what man you're talking about, Harry. But I assure you, I'm not brooding over anyone."

He made a snorting sound. "I hope your acting on the stage is better than that little performance. Otherwise, this place is going to be in big trouble."

His words brought Desiree up short. Harry was right. She'd been so caught up in her misery over Alex that she hadn't given the attention to Magnolia House she should. But that was going to change. From this moment on, Alexander Stone was history. She wasn't going to let herself think about the man another second. "You're right, Harry. I should be concentrating on the opening." Pushing away from the table, she went over to him, gave him a hug and followed through with a kiss to his cheek. "Thanks."

"Cut it out," he told her, his face and head coloring, but not before he gave her shoulder an affectionate squeeze. "You're going to make me forget why I came looking for you in the first place. I've got a message for you."

She couldn't help it. Her first thought was Alex and her double-crossing heart skipped a beat before she could check it. "A message?"

"Yeah. Kevin phoned. Says he needs to talk to you. He said he's got a big problem and needs your help."

Seven

It was no use. Alex threw down the contracts. He'd been reading the same page over and over for the past thirty minutes without making any progress. He simply couldn't concentrate. Not when Desiree's image refused to stay out of his head. It was the cottage, Alex told himself as his gaze drifted once more toward the window, seeking a glimpse of her. Sighing, he shut his eyes a moment. What man wouldn't have trouble erasing her from his thoughts? The woman was every man's fantasy come to life with her long legs and lush figure, that whiskey-soft voice and come-hither smile. It was a wonder some man hadn't already snapped her up with promises of that fairy tale she wanted. He opened his eyes on that thought. *He* certainly wasn't about to make that mistake.

Agitated, he pushed away from the desk. He should never have agreed to stay here and wait for Kevin. He should have just flown out to Chicago and tried to talk some sense into the kid instead of agreeing to meet him here.

But three days ago, it had seemed the right thing to do. While he'd been relieved to learn that the dancer Kevin had asked to marry him had refused his proposal, the rest of their conversation hadn't gone quite as well. Leaning back in his chair, Alex rubbed at his eyes and once again replayed the conversation in his head:

"I'm not sure I want to be a lawyer."

"Of course you want to be a lawyer," Alex had argued. "That's always been the plan, Kev. You get your law degree, put a year or two in at the firm and then help me to run Stone Enterprises. The company and the family need you."

"Come on, Alex. The company doesn't need me. And neither does the family. They have you."

Alex had felt a band tighten around his chest. "Kevin, if I've made you feel that you're not really needed—"

"No. It's not that. Honest. You've been great. I couldn't have asked for a better brother or friend."

"But..."

"But sometimes when I look in the mirror, I break out in a cold sweat because I see myself following in your footsteps. And don't take this wrong, Alex. You're my brother and I care about you, but no way do I want to end up like you." Releasing a deep sigh, he continued, "What I'm trying to say is that a dozen years from now, I don't want to end up with nothing to show for my life but a fat bank balance and a lot of stock options. Maybe that's enough for you, but it isn't for me. I want more."

"And by more, you mean marriage. Do you honestly think that's going to make you happy? How many times did our parents try that route, and look at the misery it caused them. And us."

"It wasn't all bad, Alex. Sometimes things were pretty

good. Those two years when Dad and Julie were married were really nice.''

It had been with his father's third wife that both boys had actually felt like part of a real family. ''But it didn't last, did it?'' And when Julie had left them, he'd never felt so alone in his life. It was then that he'd given up any hope of ever being a real family and vowed never to put himself or anyone else through that torture again.

''Just because our folks made a mess of things doesn't mean that we will, too. Not all relationships fall apart. Some of them last a lifetime.''

''But most of them don't.''

''All I know is I'm willing to take a chance. Unfortunately, Jane wasn't.''

''I'm sorry, Kev. I know you're probably hurting right now. But believe me, you're better off without her. In a couple of months when the sex began to cool down, the two of you would've been at each other's throats and wishing you'd never gotten married in the first place.''

''I guess that's something neither one of us will ever know because she did turn me down.''

He had hated to hear the pain in his brother's voice. ''Kevin—''

''Don't worry, Alex. I'll be all right. Sure, I admit it. Right now I feel like I've been kicked in the teeth. But the thing is I also feel alive. I took a risk and it didn't pan out, but at least I took that risk. At least I'm living my life, not hiding from it.''

Alex sat up straight in his office chair. Was that how Kevin saw him? As a man who was hiding from life? His brother was wrong, Alex told himself. He wasn't hiding from life. He was living it just the way he wanted. He had a thriving, challenging business, an active social life and any number of interesting females with whom he could share a meal or a movie and occasionally even his bed. What he didn't have were the roller-coaster highs and lows that went with falling in and out of love. He didn't have the messy scenes and disappointments when a relationship failed. He didn't have the broken promises and lives that came with divorce.

And he didn't have Desiree.

Restless, Alex abandoned his chair and retreated to the kitchen. He was not going to start thinking about her again, he told himself. To do so would be a waste of time. There was no way a woman like her would fit into his life, even if he wanted her to. And he didn't want her in his life. Grabbing a filter, he measured out coffee grinds. After filling the coffeepot with water, he turned the machine on.

He and Desiree had absolutely nothing in common. She was an actress in hock up to her pretty neck with a dinner theater that had, at best, five-to-one odds of succeeding. He was a businessman who'd made his first million before he turned twenty-one. She believed in fairy tales. He was as pragmatic as they came. She wanted love and happily ever afters. He didn't believe in either.

But she had the most incredibly soft mouth, he admitted as her face swam in front of him again. And a way of looking at him that made his blood churn in his veins. Alex drew a steadying breath and shook his head to clear the image. Reaching for the milk, he poured it into a pan and turned on the burner of the stove.

Hormones. That's all it was. His had been on warp speed since the first time he'd laid eyes on her. He knew what the problem was. It was a simple case of the male-female chemistry at work—hormones, pheromones. And since he knew what the problem was, he could control it.

He was a master when it came to control. Always had been. He *was* in control now. And no matter how tempting it might be, he refused to give Desiree Mason another thought. Pouring steamed milk into his cup, he added coffee. He'd simply put her out of his mind, he decided, stirring his coffee.

He took a sip.

"Damn!" Alex put the cup down on the countertop and stared at what he'd done. He took his coffee black—or at least he had before he'd met Desiree. He scrubbed a hand down his face.

You're in trouble, Stone. Big trouble.

And he had a sinking feeling it was going to get a whole lot worse.

"Come on, Des. I swear I'll be back in time for the opening. I just can't pass up this chance."

"All right, Kevin. But if you're not back next week, I'm going to replace you." That is, if she could find someone to take over his part. So far, the drama students who'd decided to hang around the city for the summer were either already working in summer stock or weren't because they had a long way to go before they'd be able to successfully carry off a role in any production.

"And you'll explain things to Alex for me?"

Desiree hesitated. "I don't like this, Kevin. Don't you think *you* should be the one to tell him? After all, he's *your* brother. I'm sure if you explained to him about getting the call-back, he'll understand."

"Ha! You obviously don't know Alex. You should have heard the riot act he read me when I told him I wanted to get married. I swear, if Jane hadn't turned down my proposal, I think Alex would have found some way to stop the wedding."

"But this is different," she reasoned. "This is about what you want to do with your life. Up to now, you've let him believe your interest in acting is nothing more than a hobby, a way to meet girls. It's time you told him the truth—that you want to be an actor, not a lawyer.''

"I *did* try to tell him, the other day when I called.''

"What did he say?''

"He argued with me, tried to convince me I was wrong. Then when I tried to explain that I didn't want to be like him, I...well, I'm not sure, but I think I might have actually hurt his feelings.''

Desiree felt that tug at her heart again. Given Alex's love for his brother, she didn't doubt for a moment that Kevin's words had hurt him.

"Please, Des. You tell him for me. He'll take the news better if it comes from you.''

She doubted that sincerely. "He and I hardly know each other. You, on the other hand, are his brother.''

"And I know my brother. It'll be a lot better if the news comes from you instead of me.''

"Why in the world would you think that?''

"Because there was something in his voice when your name came up the other night and the way he was questioning me about you. My guess is my big brother has a crush on you. Who knows? He might even fall in love with you.''

"Keep your shirt on. I'm coming.''

Alex didn't sound at all like a man who was on the verge of falling in love with her, Desiree thought, as she heard a thud followed by a swear word and then the sound of approaching feet across the cottage floor.

He yanked open the door, and Desiree stared at his naked chest. After a quick scan southward that revealed a pair of jeans and bare feet, she lifted her gaze. She swallowed. Given the scowl on his face, he didn't look like a man who even "liked" her at the moment, she decided.

Alex flipped the light switch by the door and let out an exasperated sigh when nothing happened. "Great. The bulb's burned out."

"That's all right. There's a full moon tonight." She hesitated a second, already regretting her decision to come. "I'm sorry for just showing up like this. I guess I should have called first. If this is a bad time, I can come back in the morning."

"No." He swiped a hand through his damp hair. "It's not a bad time. I'm just not in the best of moods. It's this dam—darned heat. I just finished taking a shower. Thought it might help take the edge off this heat. I don't know how the people who live here stand it."

Nerves jumping, Desiree pasted a smile on her lips. "I guess it does take a bit of getting used to."

"I don't think I could ever get used to it."

"Actually, it's not too bad right now. August is the real scorcher. In fact, tonight it's rather pleasant outside."

"Maybe."

There were shadows under his eyes, and he was in bad need of a shave. Even his usually short hair, still damp from his shower, was a bit long for him. After not seeing him for three days, even agitated, Alex looked beautiful to her. He also looked so lost and so totally unAlexlike that he stole another chunk of her heart.

Oh, sweet mercy, she really was in love with him, she realized. It wasn't that sweet-rush-of-attraction kind of love that you knew would be fun, but was never meant to last. And it wasn't that warm, pleasant feeling you experienced for someone you were genuinely fond of. No, this was the real eighteen-karat gold, knot-in-the-stomach, honest-to-goodness love. The kind of love that came with a capital L. The kind of love that wasn't going to run its course and then go away like a bad case of the flu simply because Alex didn't feel the same way.

"You all right?"

No, she wasn't all right. She was soul-deep in love with a man who didn't believe in love, a man who had no faith in happy ever afters. She was in deep, dangerous water and didn't have a clue what to do about it. "I, umm...I'm fine."

"You sure? You look a little pale. Maybe you should come inside and sit down for a moment."

"No! That's all right," she said more calmly. No way did she want to go inside that cottage again and think about the last time she'd been in there with him, the way it had felt to be in his arms, to have him kiss her, to touch her.

His dark brows scrunched together as he studied her and waited. "Was there something you wanted?"

What she wanted was *him*. She wanted him to play the leading role in her dreams for the future. She wanted the two of them to love each other, to have a lifetime together making those dreams come true. Suddenly realizing how dangerous that line of thought could be, she shut it off. "I...umm, I needed to talk to you for a few minutes. If you want to finish getting dressed first, I can wait out here on the porch."

Alex looked down at his bare chest as though he hadn't even realized he was missing his shirt and shoes. Slowly he lifted his gaze to meet hers. The air sizzled with the sexual energy flowing between them. Desiree's heart began to hammer. "On second thought, maybe it would be better if I did come back in the morning, after all."

"No. I shouldn't have left things hanging with you this long as it is. Just give me a second to grab a shirt, and I'll be right back." Leaving the door ajar, he headed for the back of the cottage. "Sure you don't want to come inside?" he called out from the bedroom.

"No, thanks. It really is nice out here. I'm enjoying

this breeze.'' She sat down on the porch swing and waited for her heartbeat to return to normal.

By the time he came back outside, Desiree's pulse had gone from a gallop to a steady trot—until she saw him. And then her heart was racing like a Thoroughbred around the track on Derby Day.

He sat down next to her on the swing and pushed off with one foot, sending the swing into a slow, lazy motion. Silence stretched between them for several long heartbeats, with only the creaking of the swing breaking the quiet. ''I'm assuming you've talked to Kevin and you know that his wedding plans are off?''

''Yes. He told me.'' She stole a glance at him. He'd put a shirt on, but hadn't bothered to finish up the buttons or tuck it into his pants. She wished to heaven he had because her gaze kept straying to that sprinkling of dark hair that ran down his chest and disappeared into the waist of his jeans. She forced her eyes back up to his face. ''He seems to be handling the rejection pretty well.''

Alex shrugged. ''Like I told him,'' he said, pushing his toes to keep the swing moving in a slow swaying motion. ''It was for the best. Getting married would have been a big mistake.''

A mistake that Alex would never make, Desiree thought sadly, as she heard the conviction in his voice. No, Alex Stone was too smart to let himself succumb to an emotion like love. Whereas she, she'd had no choice. Her feelings for him had sneaked up on her. He'd ambushed her heart with his rushing to his brother's rescue even if his brother didn't need rescuing. He'd parked himself in her heart with his soft spot for her pets despite his allergies, with his kindness a few days ago, to a neighbor's boy who'd wanted to learn to fish. Alex didn't realize just how much of that loneliness and vulnerability he'd revealed to her.

"I guess you're here about the cottage," he said. "I know I told you I was leaving and that you could go ahead and lease the place again. And that hasn't changed. I'm still planning to leave, and you're still welcome to do whatever you want when I'm gone. I meant what I said. I don't intend to try to break the lease or get any kind of a refund."

Desiree remained silent. It was a generous offer, but one she knew she couldn't accept. She'd have to see to it that Alex was refunded his money.

"Only thing is it's going to be a few more days before I leave. I promised Kevin I'd wait for him to get back." Worry lines etched across his brow as he spoke of his brother. "I'm hoping I can talk some sense into him when he gets here and get him to go back to law school."

Great, Desiree thought. And she was here to mess up those plans. How did she let herself get into these messes? But she already knew the answer. She was a sucker when it came to helping a friend. She simply had never learned the art of saying no when someone needed her. "As far as I'm concerned, you leased the cottage for a year, Alex. It's yours to use or not use for the next year. It's up to you. But the cottage isn't the reason I'm here."

He stopped pushing the swing. "Then why did you come?"

The deep growl of his voice wrapped around her like a velvet glove, sending a shiver of longing down her spine. She cut a glance to him. Moonlight fell on his face, revealing the sharp line of his jaw, his poet's mouth and those midnight eyes of his lasering in on her mouth. Her pulse jackknifed, then thudded at breakneck speed. Hopping off the swing, she retreated to the safety of the porch railing. "I, umm...I came to talk to you about Kevin."

She heard the creak of wood behind her as Alex obviously abandoned the swing. "What about him?"

She curled her fingers around the banister and kept her eyes glued to the pale yellow moon. "He called this evening, to say he wouldn't be back tomorrow like he'd planned. He's been delayed."

"How much of a delay are we talking about?"

"Not long. He'll be back sometime next week."

"Did he happen to tell you the reason for the delay?"

"The reason?" Desiree repeated, her throat suddenly dry at the sound of his voice directly behind her.

"Yes. Why isn't he coming back tomorrow?"

"He, um, he auditioned for a play and got a callback."

"He's been trying out for a play?"

"Yes."

"I see." There was a wealth of emotion in the two words. "And evidently he asked you to do his dirty work—and break the news to me."

"Yes. I mean, no. I mean..." She didn't know what she meant. How could she even think when her blood was pounding in her ears? She took a deep breath and started over. "Kevin was worried you'd be upset if he told you. He knows how you feel about him acting and that you want him to go back to law school. But the truth is, he doesn't want to be a lawyer, he wants to be an actor."

"Then Kevin needs to be man enough to tell me that himself," he snapped. "You should never have come here tonight, Desiree."

"You're right," she said, mortified that while her intentions had been good—to help a friend—she had overstepped her boundaries. "This really is between you and Kevin. I had no right to interfere."

Alex caught her shoulders, turned her around to face him. "That's not what I meant," he said, his voice angry, his expression stormy.

A breeze whispered past her, carrying the scent of night jasmine and summer rain on the way. But the heat in his gaze as Alex looked at her was like a blast of flame from a four-alarm blaze.

"I promised myself I wouldn't do this," he told her, his fingers tightening on her shoulders. "Just another couple of days and I'd have been gone. I swore to myself I'd stay away from you until then. And I thought I could keep that promise. But you had to go and screw everything up by coming here tonight. I'm all wrong for you. I can't give you those fairy-tale endings you've got your heart set on, or make you any of those promises you want. But I want you, anyway. God help me, I want you and it's driving me crazy."

"Alex, I—"

"Dammit, why couldn't you just stay away?"

She opened her mouth to tell him, to try to explain again that she realized coming here tonight had been a mistake on her part, but he never gave her a chance. Because he was seizing her mouth, capturing her lips like a warrior with a dizzying speed and hunger that had her clutching at his shirtfront to hang on. There was anger in his kiss and frustration, and a wild hunger that left her breathless. She could feel her stomach jumping, her blood spinning as he feasted on her lips.

Finally he lifted his head a fraction and cupped her face in his hands. Somewhere out there in the night she could hear frogs croaking, a bird calling its mate, a squirrel scurrying up a tree. She thought she saw a flash of heat lightning streak through the sky.

Desire ripped through her like a bolt of lightning as he lowered his head and kissed her again. She could still taste that savage need in his kiss, but this time there was no anger, no demand. This time he gave as much as he took, his mouth gentling as he rubbed his lips against hers, soothing, coaxing before he dipped inside to take long, slow tastes. He continued to kiss her, one kiss spinning into another and then another, until nothing in the world existed save the feel of his mouth on hers.

She'd known for the past three days that she was in love with him, had told herself she would get over it. She'd almost convinced herself she could do just that, until she'd come here tonight.

She ran her fingers along his whiskered jaw, slid her arms up around his neck and brought his lips back to hers. He anchored her to him as though he was afraid she would turn him away. He had no idea how much that small gesture, the desperate hunger in his kiss told her about the beastly loneliness inside him. It tore at her heart. She'd never been able to turn away any creature in need. Alex may not believe in love and happy ever afters, Desiree realized, but there was so much need in him for both. A need that she wanted to fill.

She wasn't sure if he urged her closer or if she had pulled him to her, but somehow she found herself pressed into the vee of his thighs, his arousal pressed hard and heavy and hot against her belly.

Alex tore his mouth free. His breathing was ragged, his body taut with restraint as he attempted to put some space between them. "This is a mistake. We both know that."

She answered by pressing her mouth to the opening of his shirt. She felt him shudder, and a thrill of excitement whipped through her.

"I'm warning you, Desiree. You should leave now,"

he told her, seizing the fingers she'd set loose to explore all that springy dark hair on his chest. "Leave now while you still can, before it's too late."

She kissed the big hands holding hers captive. "It's already too late," she whispered. Pulling her hands free, she fumbled to free him of his shirt. When she reached for the snap on his jeans, Alex's control broke.

A groan tore from his throat, and then his mouth was on hers again, diving, deep, deep, endlessly deep. His hands sculpted her body, palmed her spine, squeezed her bottom. He didn't seem able to get her close enough.

Another flash of heat lightning ripped through the sky. Alex didn't seem to notice. His mouth came back to hers again, drugging her with his kisses. He lifted her up into his arms, kicked open the door to the cottage and carried her inside.

Alex lost his shirt somewhere inside the front door. She kicked off her sandals as he made his way across the living room. His shoes were abandoned in the hall. He pushed open the door to the bedroom. She barely registered the cherry wood four-poster that dominated the center of the room. A ginger jar lamp bathed the room in a soft yellow glow that emphasized the intensity of Alex's expression.

He released her and allowed her feet to touch the floor. Never once taking his eyes from her, he parted the folds of her blouse. "Desiree." He whispered her name like a prayer as he uncovered her breasts. In the space of a heartbeat, her skirt and panties had joined her blouse on the floor.

She trembled under that hot, liquid gaze for a moment, and then he was dispensing with his jeans with dizzying speed, ripping back the dusky blue comforter on the bed, tossing pillows to the floor.

Then he was reaching for her, lowering her to the bed.

She ran her hands up his arms, across his sleek-muscled shoulders, along his whisker-roughened cheeks and chin. His eyes were as black as a moonless sky as he caught her hand, kissed the inside of her palm.

Desiree shivered as his mouth continued its exploration to the inside of her wrist, her elbow, her shoulder, to the hollow at her throat. He zeroed in on her mouth again, but his hands continued to roam. Her breasts ached, the tips hardened under his touch, and she could feel the fire continue to build inside her.

He tore his mouth free to taste the curve of her neck and shoulder before moving to her breast. He laved the tightened nipple with his tongue. "Alex," she cried out, arching her back. Never, never had she known desire could be like this, so hot, so wild, so wanton.

His mouth continued to taste and sample her body, finding a sensitive spot behind her knee, inside her thigh, at the curve of her hip. He made her ache. He made her want. He drove her mad with desire before he slipped his finger down to tease the bud at her center. All the while his insatiable mouth continued to make love to her breasts.

The fire inside her continued to build under those slow, steady strokes of his fingers, under that never-still mouth of his. Suddenly Desiree exploded, shattered into a thousand pieces of light as her body shivered beneath him. She'd barely caught her breath before he started the torture again. He was driving her mad, branding her body as he had already branded her heart.

She reached for him, brought his mouth back to hers and kissed him with all the love in her soul. Her heart was pounding, her blood pumping in her veins again, just as hot, just as needy as it had been moments before.

Alex lifted his head to look at her. There was a dark fire in his eyes—a fire that told her this would be no gentle loving, no simple mating. But she'd already known that. "Alex, I—"

Before she could get the words out, to tell him she loved him, he swooped down and took her mouth again before he moved between her legs.

"Look at me, Desiree," he whispered as he parted her with his fingers. "I need to see your eyes." Then he was entering her, driving deep and hard.

Desiree wrapped her legs around him, drawing him deeper inside her, giving him all that he demanded, giving him all that she had to give.

His eyes remained steady on her face as he took them closer and closer to the edge of that dangerous cliff. She watched the walls of control Alex had clung to begin to tumble, and in that split second while they teetered on the precipice, she saw the naked yearning and need in his eyes. She wanted to answer that need. Arching her hips once more, she wrapped her body tightly around his and gave him her heart.

Her body shuddered first. Then she heard Alex call out her name just before he convulsed and took them plunging over the cliff and into the fires below. "I love you, Alex," she cried out, holding on to him as the flames wrapped around them and forged them into one.

Eight

Making love to her had been a mistake.

Alex knew it in his bones, could feel it in his gut. He'd told himself a hundred times he wasn't going to become involved with her. He'd sworn he was going to stay away from her. And he'd meant to. Heaven help him, he'd meant to. He truly had.

But he hadn't counted on her showing up here tonight—not while the image of her coming apart in his arms, the feel of her body beneath his hands, had plagued him day and night for three solid days. Not while desire had him clenched by the throat like an angry beast demanding to be fed.

One glimpse at her, standing there in the moonlight, looking so damned beautiful and unsure of herself as she apologized to him, and all of his good intentions had turned to spit. He knew the precise moment sanity had deserted him—when he'd caught that brief tremble of her lower lip before she pasted on that phony smile. Then he'd lost it. He'd been unable to walk away.

And he should have walked away, Alex told himself. The two of them played by different rules, had different expectations. She had dreams of white picket fences and fairy-tale endings. While he, he had no expectations, no hope for something more, because he knew what a mistake that could be. He knew where all those expectations would lead. Hadn't he witnessed it time and again with his own parents? How often had he seen it happen with his friends? How many times had he watched the flurry of plans and promises made during that first bloom of love and lust give way to hurt, to disillusionment, to broken dreams.

He should have walked away from her, Alex told himself. But he hadn't. And now... Alex looked at the woman he held in his arms with her head resting on his shoulder, her hair fanned out across his arm. He wove his fingers through those silky red-gold tresses. Something warm and tender stirred inside him. It seemed so natural to be here with her, to hold her like this, he thought.

Suddenly his fingers stilled. Panic shot through him like a bullet at the direction of his thoughts. In the past, his feelings for a woman had generally been limited to lust. He didn't want to feel anything more for Desiree.

And he wouldn't, Alex promised himself. He'd learned a lifetime ago how to control his emotions. He would do so now with Desiree and save them both a lot of heartache in the long run. Feeling calmer at his decision, he focused on the problem of making sure she understood.

The "problem" in his arms chose that moment to shift one of her legs across his. She snuggled closer, her hand and soft breast pressing against his side. Desire stirred inside him again, making him ache. Biting back the urge to stroke his hand along her hip, he closed his eyes. Making love to her had definitely been a mistake. It had also been incredible. And was a true test of his willpower because he desperately wanted to make love to her again now.

"Hmm."

Alex opened his eyes as Desiree stretched out like a lazy cat before cuddling closer and pressing her body more intimately against his. Looking at her had been another mistake, he realized, as he fought against the craving to slide that smooth, sleek body of hers beneath his and bury himself in her heat once more.

He swallowed. To do so would be insane. It would only make matters more difficult than they already were, because he knew he was going to hurt her. He didn't want to, hated to do so, in fact. But he would hurt her all the same. It didn't matter that he'd warned her, that he'd tried to tell her and she had been the one who'd chosen to stay. He'd known almost from the start where this would lead—with her thinking she loved him and him unable to love her back. He should have been smart enough to figure out a way to prevent it.

He shifted his gaze up to the ceiling, needing to look at anything but the tempting sight of Desiree naked in his arms. The lamplight cast a blurred shadow of their bodies above the bed. He stared at the fuzzy reflection of their intertwined forms. Just like love, he told himself. Love was no more than a shadow that would disappear with the light.

Desiree moved beside him again, and Alex nearly groaned. He could feel his resolve quickly turning to dust with each shift of her body. Her fingers moved lazily down his chest, easing their way to his hip. A breath shuddered through him as she continued her exploration, bringing him dangerously near the edge of his control.

She pressed a kiss to his chest, and he felt himself slip a bit deeper.

"I love you," she murmured.

The words struck him like a blast of ice water in the face. Guilt slammed at him, hitting fast and hard like a prizefighter's punch. He yanked on the reins of his control. He couldn't do this to her. He wouldn't, he told himself, and caught her questing fingers.

After several moments of silence in which he struggled with what to say to her, she said, "It's all right, Alex. You can put away the boxing gloves."

"Boxing gloves?" he repeated.

She tugged her fingers free and reached up to touch his cheek. She turned his face toward her. "My guess is you're lying here beating yourself up and feeling guilty because we made love."

Her voice was whisper soft and smoky and did strange things to his pulse. Alex swallowed, disliking the fact that she could affect him so easily. "You're very good at reading a person's thoughts. Maybe you're some kind of a witch or sorceress."

Desiree sighed. Withdrawing her hand, she reached for the sheet and pulled it up around her body, then propped herself up on her elbow to look down at him. "It doesn't take a witch to figure out that you regret making love with me. Because you do regret it, don't you?"

Regret making love to her? Not in this lifetime, he wouldn't. How could he ever regret something so extraordinary? He'd made love to other women, but none of those experiences had prepared him for what lovemaking would be like with her. No one else had even come close to making him feel the way she did. And it frightened him at just how soul-deep that connection to her had felt, at how tempted he was to forget his own rules. But he couldn't. And he couldn't tell her those things. Because if he did, he'd be breaking another of his rules—he'd be giving her hope for a future with him when there was none. He knew what kind of man he was—a realist, not a dreamer and believer in fairy tales. Desiree needed a man who could at least try to believe in those fairy tales with her. That man wasn't Alex.

"I'm right, aren't I? You think it was a mistake."

"It *was* a mistake."

She tipped up her chin and met his gaze squarely. "Why? Because I told you I love you?"

"No." He shifted up onto his elbow to look at her. "What happened between us was…" He searched for the right words to try to tell her how much making love to her had meant to him and all the reasons it would be a mistake for it to happen again. "It was…"

"*Spectacular?*" she offered with a smile. "Or what about *wonderful?* Or maybe *fantastic* would be better?" He could see the nerves behind her smile, behind that light tone she was trying to convey. "I've got it. How about all of the above?"

"I'm trying to be serious, Desiree."

"So am I." She leaned over and pressed a kiss to his mouth. "You were wonderful, Alex. If I'd been wearing socks, you'd have knocked them right off."

"Desiree—"

She touched a finger to his lips. "We made love, Alex. And for me it was a pretty fantastic experience, one I'd like to repeat often. Let's not spoil it by analyzing it to death and making it out to be more than it was."

The woman was dangerous, Alex told himself. He could feel his conviction weakening as she eased him back down onto the bed. It cost him, cost him dearly, but Alex snagged the hands that were already making their way from his shoulders to his chest and headed for his belly. He kept his eyes fastened on her face and not on the sheet slipping down her body. "And just what is it you think happened between us?"

She hesitated, uncertainty flickered in her eyes for a second as though she suspected him of asking her a trick question. Then she pasted another of what was obviously meant to be a nonchalant smile on her lips. "I think we've started an affair."

"An affair."

"Yes. I believe that's what you call it when two people become...when they become involved sexually. Or am I wrong? Maybe there's some cool new word being used to describe it now that I don't know about."

"Not that I know of. I suppose 'affair' is the term most people would use to describe this situation. But I doubt it's the one you would use."

She narrowed her eyes. "What do you mean?"

"I mean for you I think what happened between us would mean a lot more than just two people having sex. For you it would mean being in love, having a relationship, planning a future together."

She tugged for him to release her hands, but Alex held on to her wrists. "Honestly, Alex, how did you get all of that out of a few little words said while I was in the throes of passion? I tell people I love them all the time—Harry, Charlie, even Kevin. If you'll remember, just a week ago you yourself believed I was in love with your brother and planning to marry him."

He remembered. And he also discovered that a big part of his problem with that idea had been that he wanted Desiree for himself. The other thing he'd learned was that while she might be generous with her affection, that affection was no less sincere. And that's what scared him. That she really did believe she was in love with him. "What I remember is that I was an idiot."

"And you're being an idiot again right now." She tried to jerk her hands free, but he held her steady.

"Did you mean it?"

She stopped struggling and looked up at him. "I..."

"Did you mean it, Desiree?" He rolled her onto her back and pinned her with his body. "Did you mean it when you said you loved me?"

"Yes."

A wave of satisfaction rushed through him, shocking him that her admission mattered so much to him. He remembered the nerve-shattering experience of having her say those words to him while he'd lost himself in her. As though his body was remembering that pleasure, too, Alex suddenly became aware of the fact that they were lying naked together, with only a thin sheet separating their bodies. The blood roared in his veins as he took in the pearl colored skin of her throat, inhaled the scent he'd come to think of as hers—wildflowers and moonlight and some exotic floral spice that made him think of seduction and sin. Her nipples puckered against the sheet. He could feel her heartbeat picking up speed. But it didn't come close to matching the fast pace of his own. He wanted desperately to rip away the sheet and lose himself in her again.

"Alex?"

The husky murmur of his name on her lips sent a shudder of anticipation through him. He knew what she was asking. He could see the question in her eyes. She wanted him to make love to her again. Because she thought she was in love with him. And she wanted him to love her back. She didn't understand, as he did, that love was nothing more than a chemical game. It was nature's way of ambushing mankind by tricking them into believing that physical attraction was more than it was. If he made love to her now, he'd be taking the love she offered and giving nothing in return. No, he refused to use her that way. He rolled off her and onto his back. He rested his arm across his eyes. "I don't want your love, Desiree."

There was a heartbeat of silence and then she said, "I'm afraid your wanting or not wanting me to love you has little bearing on the matter. It doesn't change the fact that I do."

He flung his arm away from his eyes to stare at her. "Don't waste it on me, because I don't love you and I have no intention of fooling myself into thinking that I do."

"I see," she whispered, but there was no hiding the pain in her eyes as she tucked the sheet more closely to her. She wrapped her arms around her body as though she was suddenly chilled.

"I doubt that you do. Like most people, you'll go to your grave still believing in those fairy tales of yours about love and hoping that they'll someday come true. I want no part of that merry-go-round. I've seen the damage it can do and I swore a long time ago I'd never be a part of it. I don't intend to start now."

"Loving someone doesn't have to be a bad thing. Not with the right person."

"And you think that maybe you're the right person?"

Tears swam in her eyes, but she met his gaze evenly. "I could be. I think you feel something for me, and if given a chance it could grow into more."

He could feel it again, that heavy weight crushing his chest, that sick twisting in his gut that what she said might just be true. Suddenly he thought of his parents, the incredible highs that surrounded their lives with each new relationship they started and the wrenching despair that followed when the relationships failed. Most of all he could remember his own sense of loss and abandonment when the people he'd come to trust and care for disappeared from his life. He refused to let that happen to him again. "You're wrong," he told her, feeling like pond scum for hurting her. "What I feel for you is lust. Not love. I don't love you and I'm never going to fall in love with you."

Pain flashed in her eyes, turning them a deep, dark green. Keeping the sheet tucked around her, she eased from the bed and began gathering up her clothes.

It was crazy, Alex told himself, a sense of dread building inside him as he watched her pick up her things. He didn't want her to go, he realized. Hell, he wanted to drag her back to the bed and make love to her again and again until he could wipe out the icy fear burning at the back of his throat. "Desiree." He called her name as she reached the bedroom door.

She turned back to look at him, and the expression on her face was as fragile as glass. He'd hurt her...badly. He swore silently, angry with himself. "I'm sorry."

She shrugged. "Don't worry about it. If your theory is right, my loving you is like a bad case of the flu. A couple of days, a week at best, and I'll be over it."

Alex had been wrong. Love wasn't like the flu, Desiree decided as she separated another Oreo cookie. "Uh-hmm. I understand," she said. Propping the phone between her ear and shoulder, she listened to her sister Clea explain why she couldn't make it in from Chicago for the dinner theater's grand opening.

It had been thirteen days since Alex had packed his bags and returned to Boston, Desiree mused as she scooped the crème out of the center of the cookie with her finger and stuck it into her mouth. And she was no closer to getting over him now than she had been that first night.

"I'm really sorry, Des. But every one of our travel

agents is already booked up for the weekend. Now that the doctor has confined Nancy to bed for the rest of her pregnancy, I'm going to have to cover all of her tours until I can find someone to replace her.''

"It's OK, Clea. I understand.'' She broke off a piece of the dark chocolate cookie and popped it into her mouth. Once more her thoughts strayed back to Alex. She hadn't known falling in love with someone could hurt so much. She still wasn't sure how she'd managed to gather up her clothes and walk out of the cottage that night when inside she'd felt as though a knife had just been rammed through her heart. Another stab of pain slashed through her as she recalled Alex telling her that he didn't want her love.

"You're sure you're OK about my not coming?'' Clea asked.

"Uh-hmm.'' She finished off the other half of the cookie. No, getting over loving Alexander Stone was definitely not as simple as getting over the flu. But then some flu cases turned out to be terminal, and judging by how banged up she was feeling inside, she was beginning to suspect loving Alex would prove to be a terminal case, too.

"I'd be there if I could. You know that, don't you?''

"Uh-hmm,'' she replied absently and contemplated eating another cookie.

"I was really looking forward to coming. The truth is, I could do with a little time away from here.''

Desiree paused, all thoughts of another cookie gone at the troubled note in her sister's voice. "Clea, is everything all right there?''

"Sure. Everything's fine. Just busy,'' her sister said, the I-can-handle-anything tone returning to her voice. "Business is booming.''

No news flash there, Desiree decided. Her sister was

smart, focused and as shrewd as a fox when it came to managing things and people. Clea had been born to run a business and could probably even run the country if she put her mind to it. Apparently she was doing a bang-up job for the travel agency that employed her. Still, there had been something in her sister's voice...something in her tone that she could have sworn had bordered on fear.

"What about you? You must be a nervous wreck with the opening just a couple of days away."

"Not a wreck exactly. But I admit, I am a little nervous," Desiree replied, her thoughts shifting to her own business. The truth was she'd been so miserable over the way things had turned out with Alex that she hadn't been as focused as she should have been on the dinner theater's grand opening.

And this sitting around moping over Alex had to stop, Desiree told herself. Alex may not want her love, but he definitely needed it. Everyone needed to be loved by someone. If the man was too darn stubborn to see that she was good for him, that they could be good together, then it would be his loss—not hers. Besides, brooding over him wasn't doing her a lick of good, anyway. She'd been doing just fine before Alexander Stone had come into her life, Desiree reminded herself. She'd be fine again without him.

Just one more cookie, she promised herself. She filched another Oreo cookie from the bag and separated it. She wasn't going to waste another minute thinking about Alex, because if she didn't stop stuffing herself with comfort foods soon, she was going to end up comforting herself right out of her costume. And then what would happen to her dinner theater?

"How are the advance reservations coming?" Clea asked.

"Good." They were more than good, Desiree admitted. They had far exceeded her expectations. She scraped her finger through the crème filling and licked the sugar-laden mixture from her finger. "It looks like we'll be sold out for all three performances this weekend."

"That's great. It sounds like that advertising paid off."

"Looks that way. Thanks for looking over the figures for me. My head was dizzy with all those numbers and options."

"No need to thank me. In case you've forgotten, I have a vested interest in Magnolia House, and it's just as important to me as it is to you that it be a success."

"It will be," Desiree assured her.

"Then I take it you're no longer having a problem with Alex Stone."

So much for putting the man out of her thoughts, Desiree decided. She put down the mutilated cookie and rubbed at her temple. She could feel a headache coming on. She wished she'd never mentioned to Clea that Alex had shown up here in the first place. "No. He's gone back to Boston."

"Then that's good news. Right?"

"Sure."

"You know, Des, for a woman who a month ago wanted to wring the man's neck, you don't exactly sound thrilled about him being gone. I thought you said he was driving you crazy and you wanted him to leave."

"Of course I'm glad he's gone. And he *was* driving me crazy. It's just that I wish…" She swallowed, mortified by the crack in her voice. "I just wish I'd never met him in the first place."

There was a moment's silence on the other end of the line. "All right, Desiree. What's going on? And don't tell me you don't know what I'm talking about. You sound like you're about to start bawling any second. What did Stone do to you?"

At her silence, Clea went into her bossy, big-sister mode. "Answer me. What did that jerk to do you? Did he threaten you? Is that it? Because if he did, I swear I'll have my attorney slap him with a harassment suit so fast, it'll make his head spin."

"No. It's nothing like that. It's personal," Desiree told her.

"Personal?"

"Yes. Personal. I don't want to talk about it."

"How personal?" Clea asked, obviously paying no attention to her.

"Personal as in I'm not going to tell you. Forget about it, Clea. In fact, forget I ever mentioned Alex Stone." She certainly was going to do her best to try to forget him. "Listen, I have to go now."

"Desiree…"

"I'll talk to you soon."

"Desiree Mason, don't you dare hang up on me. Tell me right now what's wrong."

"Nothing's wrong, and I really do have to go. I've scheduled a dress rehearsal for two o'clock and it's almost that now and I still need to get ready. I'll call you after the opening and let you know how everything goes."

Hanging up the phone, Desiree pressed a hand to her chest, wishing she could just make the aching inside her stop. A tear slid down her cheek, and she swiped at it. After another moment she drew a deep breath and released it. *That's it, Alex Stone. I absolutely refuse to spend another minute thinking about you.* Standing, she turned her back on the cookies and headed for her room to dress for rehearsal.

"Des, you got a minute?" Kevin asked a few minutes later as she started for the ballroom to meet the cast for rehearsal. "I need to talk to you."

Desiree stopped in the middle of the corridor, Kevin's serious tone making her uneasy. "Don't you dare tell me you have to leave town again. If you do, I swear I'm going to have to kill you."

"Hey, I wouldn't run out on you now—not with the place opening this weekend."

Feeling slightly calmer, she resumed walking. "Sorry. I guess I'm getting a bit paranoid and worrying something will go wrong. All right, so what did you need to talk about?"

"Alex."

So much for her vow not to think about Alex anymore, Desiree decided as Kevin walked beside her. "Kevin, if this is about the battle you and he have been having over whether or not you should go back to law school, as much as I adore you, I really don't want to get in the middle of this. You really need to talk to Alex yourself."

"I know. That's what I plan to do, but I thought maybe I should let you know that I've asked Alex to come for the grand opening. I thought maybe if he could see me on stage…I mean, if he could see that I have some talent and that acting isn't just some whim on my part, then maybe he wouldn't think what I'm doing is such a waste."

"It's what *you* think that's important."

"I know, but, well, Alex has been more like a father to me than a brother, and I guess…I guess I'd like his approval. Anyway, I asked him to come and he said he would."

Desiree swallowed. She pressed a hand to her jittery stomach. "Then I'm glad for you. I hope things work out for you the way you want them to. Make sure he's given one of the best seats available."

"Thanks. I knew you'd understand. That's why I suggested he come early and just plan to stay at the cottage for—''

Desiree stopped and whipped around to look at Kevin. ''Alex is going to stay in the cottage?''

''Yeah.'' Kevin gave her a puzzled look. ''What is it with you two? It makes perfect sense to me. My place is too small, and it would be crazy for him to go there, anyway, when he could just stay here. I know you sent him a refund check for the balance of his lease, but you told me he sent it back. Since he's paid for the place, anyway, I thought it made sense for him to use it.''

''You're right, of course,'' Desiree told him, regaining some of her composure. ''Alex is certainly welcome to use the cottage. As you've pointed out, he's already paid for the privilege, anyway.''

Kevin flinched. ''Geez, I sure hope I didn't sound that pompous.''

Her mind still whirling at the prospect of seeing Alex again, Desiree blinked as she realized what Kevin had said. ''I'm sorry.'' She reached out to squeeze his arm. ''Don't pay any attention to me. Like you said, I haven't been myself lately.''

''No. You haven't.'' He paused and gave her a considering look. ''What in the world happened between you and Alex?''

She looked up at him. ''What makes you think something happened?''

''Come on, I know I've been kind of out of it since I came back from Chicago, I mean with Jane tossing my proposal back in my face the way she did and then not getting that role, I guess it knocked some of the wind out of my sails. Guess that's why I haven't exactly been my usual perceptive self.''

''Oh, Kevin,'' Desiree said at his reference to his broken love affair. She'd been so caught up in her own misery, she hadn't given nearly as much thought as she should to what her friend was going through. Not only had he not gotten the part he'd tried out for, but he'd been dumped by the woman he loved because marriage hadn't fit into her plans. She touched his arm. "I'm really sorry that things didn't work out for you the way you had hoped."

"Yeah. Me, too. But, hey—" He shrugged. A wicked grin curved his lips. "That means I'm free for some other lucky girl to snatch up."

"Yes, you are," she assured him with a smile. "And you'll be quite a catch."

"Yeah, I think so, too," he told her with a touch of that arrogance she had noted in his older brother. "But that's another story. We were talking about you and my brother and what happened between you two."

Desiree looked away from Kevin's suddenly shrewd eyes. "I can't imagine what makes you think anything happened between Alex and me."

He stroked his jaw and gave her a considering look. "Maybe the fact that Alex wasn't here when I got back from Chicago, after saying he would be. Knowing my brother, I can't imagine anything short of an alien invasion or a nuclear war that would've made him pass up the chance to deliver face-to-face that lecture about 'why I should go back to law school.'"

"He's a busy man. I'm sure he just needed to get back to his business."

Kevin shook his head. "Nope. That's not it. Alex may be a successful businessman with a dozen different irons in the fire at one time, but he's never let any of them come before me. I always came first for him, and he made sure I knew that the entire time I was growing up. Besides telling me, he showed me how important I was to him. He made sure we spent time together. You know, doing father-son kind of things like going to ball games, fishing, bowling. That kind of stuff. I think he was worried I'd feel abandoned or something because of the way my parents sort of dumped me on him when I was a kid. Anyway, he made a point of letting me know that he was always there for me. Business, his personal life, everything else could wait if I had a problem or needed him.''

Kevin dragged a hand through his hair as though embarrassed by how much he had revealed to her. But none of it came as a surprise. She'd already figured out that beneath all that bluster, Alex was a softie at heart. It had been obvious in his devotion to his brother. Seeing him sneak treats to Maggie and Brick and the other members of her menagerie, even though he was allergic to them, had told her volumes about the type of man he was. A kind man. A caring man.

"What I'm trying to say is that even though I didn't have a problem or need any help, Alex thought I did. That's why he came here in the first place. That's why he was waiting for me to get back. But he left without ever seeing me.'' He looked her squarely in the eyes. "The only reason I could come up with for him doing that was you.''

"Me?''

"Come on, Desiree. I know something happened between you two. I thought something was going on between you guys when I talked to you on the phone. At the time I just figured you two had clashed. I mean you're not exactly each other's type.''

Desiree nearly groaned. She didn't need to be reminded just how unsuitable the two of them were. Alex had done his best to make that clear.

"But now...now I'm not so sure that's what went down.''

"Take my word for it, Kevin. We definitely clashed heads," Desiree assured him.

"Yeah, I bet you did. But that still doesn't explain Alex leaving the way he did. Or why instead of you being all keyed up and excited about the opening of Magnolia House, you've been moping around as though your mind was a million miles away."

Desiree flushed. She turned away from Kevin. Had she been so transparent? Had everyone figured out that she'd fallen in love with Alex and he didn't feel the same way? Some actress she turned out to be. She looked out at the table and chairs that had been placed all around the ballroom. Three nights from now they would be filled with people—people who had come to see her perform. But even that thought did nothing to lift her spirits.

"If it's any consolation, from the sound of him, I'd say Alex is feeling about as lousy as you seem to be. Maybe even worse. Because just the mention of your name and the tension was so thick over the phone line, I swear you could've cut it with a knife."

"Really, Kevin—"

He tipped up her chin before she could turn away and searched her eyes. She nearly cringed because she knew what he would see there.

"Oh, man, am I dense or what?" He smacked his palm against his forehead. "You're in love with him, aren't you? You're in love with Alex."

What was the point of denying it? "Yes," she told him. "But don't worry. I intend to get over it."

Nine

Coming back here had been a mistake, Alex told himself. Giving up any pretense of sleeping, he glanced at the clock. Just after midnight and he still had the rest of tonight, not to mention the next two days and nights, to get through, without breaking down and giving in to the urge to go to Desiree and ask her for another chance.

Disgusted, he sat up on the edge of the bed and drove his hands through his hair. How had he expected to sleep here, in the same bed where he had made love to her? It was insane to even think that he could. Pushing to his feet, he grabbed his jeans and pulled them on, then shoved his feet into his shoes. He reached for his shirt and headed for the front of the cottage. He had to get out of here, to escape the images of Desiree lying beside him in that bed, her arms wrapped around him, whispering that she loved him as her body shuddered in release.

Not bothering with the light, he walked through the

den and nearly tripped over a lump on the floor. He flicked on the lamp. The jacket he had thrown on the chair when he'd come in was now lying on the floor, a ball of black fur curled up on top of it. "What are you doing here?" he asked and stooped down to scratch the little cat behind her ear. "I wonder if your mistress knows about your secret door to this place?"

"Meow," Maggie replied as though in answer to his question. She made another mewing sound, then gave him a bored look before snuggling down into his twelve-hundred-dollar designer jacket and going back to sleep.

Straightening, Alex walked over to the window and looked out at the storm raging outside the cottage. He could hear the steady drum of rain as it beat against the roof, slapped against the windows. A bolt of lightning ripped through the sky, washing the landscape in a burst of white light before it faded and returned once more to black. Thunder rumbled angrily in the distance.

Restless, Alex yanked open the door and stepped outside onto the porch. Rain swept across the gallery, splattering him with big fat drops. The wind howled like a savage wolf as it whipped through the trees and sent leaves and flowers scattering across the ground like dead soldiers. An accurate barometer of how he was feeling, Alex thought as he stared out into the dark, storm-ravaged night.

He stood there for several minutes with the wind and rain thrashing around him, and the restlessness continued to churn inside him. Then he heard it—a soft sound, a woman's voice, he realized, calling out for someone.

Alex jerked his head to the right and peered out into the darkness. He was still squinting, trying to see exactly where the sound had come from when lightning streaked through the sky again, bathing her in a shimmer of gold light.

Desiree.

Desire twisted in his gut at the sight of her less than five yards away running through the trees like some wood nymph. "Maggie! Maggie, where are you, baby?"

Alex squeezed his eyes shut for a moment against the sight of the rain-soaked nightgown clinging to her body, her hair falling wild and wet down her neck and back. Opening his eyes, he watched her race toward the gazebo. "Maggie! Maggie, where are you?"

She was a temptress, a siren come to life, and if he valued his sanity he had to resist her. But just as the sailors of old were drawn to the song of the sirens that lured their ships to the rocks, Alex was drawn to her. He stepped off the porch into the rain and followed her.

"Maggie, sweetie, please. Where are you?" She stooped down in front of the gazebo and looked beneath a loosened board. She stood up again. Shoving her dripping hair away from her face, she swung her gaze from one end of the wooden structure to the other. "Come on, baby, where are you? We need to get back to the house and out of this rain."

Suddenly, as though she'd somehow realized she was no longer alone, her body stilled. Slowly she turned around to face him. "Alex."

The sound of his name on her lips was as warm as a caress, as soft and sensual as silk. Too late he realized the mistake he'd made in following her, because now he didn't have the strength to walk away from her—not tonight. Emerging from the shadows, he started toward her.

Desiree pressed her hand to her throat, unable to breathe as she watched Alex step out of the thicket of trees. She hadn't expected to see him—not yet, not for another two days. The rain and wind whipped around him as he headed toward her, sending the tails of his unbut-

toned shirt slapping against his ribs and chest. He looked
like a Viking god, a warrior come to life, Desiree
thought, as she took in the broad shoulders, the dark hair
plastered against his head. Rain sluiced over his rugged
cheekbones, across the grim line of his mouth, down the
sharp edge of his jaw.

He came to a halt a few inches before her. The rain
continued to fall, streaming over her face and body. The
wind whistled and moaned around her, wrapping the
folds of her sodden nightgown about her ankles. Leaves
skittered across the ground, clung to her bare feet. Still,
she was unable to move. Not with Alex's gaze riveted
on her.

Her pulse scrambled as he continued to look at her.
The sheer, white nightgown that had been so soft and
cool when she had slipped it on to go to sleep had been
reduced to a clinging length of thin, wet silk. She felt
naked, vulnerable, exposed.

A bolt of lightning sliced through the sky, illuminating
Alex's face. Her heart sputtered, then began to thunder
as she looked into those midnight eyes.

"Desiree."

She swallowed at the depth of longing in his voice,
the hungry need in those diamond-hard eyes. She wanted
to run. She wanted to fling herself into his arms. She did
neither. "I…I didn't realize you were here. I didn't think
you were coming until the weekend."

"I didn't want to come back. I told myself I didn't
want to see you again."

"I see," she said, hurt because for a moment she'd
been so sure he'd changed his mind about them. Instead
he simply reconfirmed the painful truth—that he didn't
want her. He didn't love her. She wrapped her arms
around herself, suddenly feeling foolish standing out in
the midst of a storm drenched and half-naked.

"I doubt that you do, understand, I mean, because I'll be damned if I do."

Another gust of wind sent a length of wet hair slapping across her cheek. She pushed it aside. "I need to go find Maggie," she said, eager to escape.

He reached out to stay her movement. "She's at the cottage," he told her, then lifted his hand to cup her cheek.

The air backed up into her lungs at the feel of his fingers on her skin. So much for telling herself she could forget him, Desiree mocked. Forgetting how to breathe would be easier.

"I tried to stay away from you."

The admission sounded as though it had been torn from him. Heedless of the storm, Desiree couldn't have walked away from him now even if her life had depended on it.

"I swore to myself I *would* stay away and wouldn't see you again. And I tried. Lord knows I tried to keep that promise. But I haven't been able to eat or sleep or even think of anything but *you*."

Her poor Alex. His admission was filled with so much emotion, such fierce need, that had been capped tightly for too long. And now all that need and emotion was threatening to explode—just like the storm. He needed her. Whether he knew it or not, her Alex needed her. To love him. To teach him that love could be a good thing, not something hurtful and to be feared. Surrendering to that need, she turned her face into his palm and kissed him.

Alex shuddered. He closed his eyes for the briefest of seconds before they snapped open again. Then suddenly he pulled her to him. With one arm anchoring her to him, he tipped her head back and traced her mouth with his

free hand. "For two solid weeks all I could think of, all
I wanted was *this*."

Then he swooped down and took possession of her
mouth. She held on to him as he dove in, kissing her
deep and long, setting off a storm inside her that rivaled
the one going on around them. He feasted on her mouth
like a starving man. The rain was cool as it continued to
pour down over them. Moments ago she'd been chilled,
but now in Alex's arms her skin felt fire hot.

When he finally raised his head, she was clinging to
him, no longer sure she could stand on her own two feet.
As though he could read her thoughts, Alex lifted her up
in his arms and carried her up the steps and inside the
gazebo.

She knew the rain continued to pummel the roof. She
knew the wind continued to thrash at the whimsical structure, sending sheets of rain dancing through the open
windows to swirl around them. She knew all those things,
but could barely make out the sounds of the storm going
on around her for the loud pounding of her own heart.

Alex's eyes never left her face as he sat down on a
bench with her in his lap. Framing her wet face with his
hands, he lowered his head and went back to work on
her mouth.

She was drowning. Desiree was sure of it, as he kissed
her and kissed her until she thought she would die from
the pleasure of his mouth and tongue rubbing against
hers. Then he shifted his attention to her ear. Her breath
hitched as his teeth closed over the tip of one lobe. She
could feel his shaft pressing against her bottom, and desire tightened in her belly. He moved from her ear to her
neck and slowly, torturously, made his way to her throat.

He continued his journey of her with his mouth. When
he flicked his tongue over the sheer material covering the
tip of her breast, Desiree shivered. "Alex, please," she

cried out as he closed his teeth over the nipple and suckled her through the wet silk.

She curled her fingers in his hair and pulled his face up so she could see his eyes. The band around her heart tightened at the hunger and desperation she saw there. He was a man who reined in his emotions, who controlled his passions. But he'd been pushed to the edge for too long, and the brakes he'd applied to his needs failed him.

Desire fisted inside her, and Desiree pulled his mouth to hers. She kissed him, diving in deep, then deeper still. She could hear another gust of wind sweeping through the gazebo like an angry beast, but it in no way matched the storm of emotions and needs raging inside her.

As though he were caught in the same storm, Alex pulled his mouth free. He had the look of a ravaging warrior as he attacked the buttons at the front of her nightgown and peeled back the wet silk. "You're so beautiful," he whispered. He circled the nipples of each breast with his fingers, then repeated the motion with his tongue.

Her breath grew fast and shallow. So did his. Closing her eyes, she arched her back as he licked and nipped at her breasts. Desiree could feel herself growing damp and hot. She squirmed on his lap, clutched his shoulders as she felt his manhood, rock hard and heavy, pressing against the thin lace of her panties.

Alex slid his hands down her waist, swept them over her hips to the tops of her knees. She heard the ragged sound of his breathing and opened her eyes to look at his face. There was desire in his eyes, savage and burning hot. There was also emotion—a fierce longing that was more than physical.

"I want you, Desiree. I have no right. But I want you just the same."

There were nerves behind that admission. And she suspected fear—fear of accepting that she loved him, fear of loving her in return. Her poor Alex. He so needed love in his life. She could see that, even if he didn't. And if she told him she loved him again, he'd probably bolt like an angry tiger.

So she tried to show him instead. She kissed him—starting with his mouth—trying to show him all the love in her heart for him. She moved to his jaw, then on to the pulse beating frantically in his neck. Still not satisfied, she pushed the shirt off his tense shoulders, dragged the sleeves down his arms before returning to those strong, hard shoulders. She kissed the rain-dampened muscles and then moved to his chest. She closed her teeth over one flat, male nipple.

She caught his sharp intake of breath. He went dead still for the length of a heartbeat and then he grabbed her hands. He pulled them up to circle his neck. Swooping down, he claimed her mouth. And then he kissed her as she had kissed him—long and hard and deep. When he pulled his mouth free, she'd barely had time to catch her breath before he was shifting her from his lap. He leaned her back against the bench, slid his hands up her thighs. In the blink of an eye, he'd rid her of the scrap of lace. She shivered as he tested her with his fingers and found her damp and ready.

A crack of thunder shook the gazebo. Or perhaps it was the roar of blood in her veins. She fumbled with the snap of his jeans, battled with the zipper. Finally she heard the hiss of metal on metal.

Alex muttered something, a curse or a prayer, she wasn't sure which. Her blood spinning, she stroked his hardened length. He groaned, the sound a ragged cry seemingly torn from deep inside him. Then he was all speed—hard, dangerous kisses and eager, hungry hands.

His eyes never left her face as he moved between her thighs, wrapped her legs around his waist and drove himself inside her.

She linked her hands with his and took him inside her, deeply, completely, without hesitation. That look of uncertainty slipped from his face and he took what she offered, gave himself in return.

He loved her. She was sure of it. She sensed it in the way he deliberately slowed things down as though he wanted to savor each moment. It was there in the tenderness of his kisses, the gentle stroking of his hands. This was more than a physical joining, more than just sex. It was a fusing of hearts, a fusing of two souls into one. Their bodies moved together like words and music joining to create a new song.

The storm played out its furious tune all around them with crashing thunder and arrows of lightning. The wind added to the chorus, whipping through the windows, driving rain and the scent of night jasmine inside the gazebo.

Rain sprayed over her, icy cold on her bare skin, but Alex's hands and mouth were fire hot and loving as they streaked over her. Together they moved in unison to the quickening tempo of the storm.

And when the explosion came, the release ripped through her like lightning and sent her hurtling with Alex into the dark, storm-filled night.

The storm had ended more than an hour ago. Moonlight spilled through the window, bathing the room in a soft, hushed glow. Lying on her back, Desiree gazed up at the ceiling, feeling a similar glow inside herself.

Somehow they'd managed to make it from the gazebo back to the cottage and into Alex's bed. He'd made love to her there a second time, slowly, tenderly, never taking

his eyes off her face as though he were trying to record
each sigh, each murmur that passed between them for
safekeeping. Which was sweet, but silly, Desiree decided
as she smiled to herself. She wasn't going to disappear.
They'd have a lifetime, several lifetimes of memories to
make together.

Unless she'd been wrong.

Unless Alex hadn't had a change of heart.

She'd been so caught up in the excitement and heat of
the moment, of being with him again, having him confess
he'd been unable to stay away, that she hadn't considered
she might be wrong. What if nothing had changed? Suppose he still didn't want her in his life?

Anxiety settled like a lead weight in the pit of her
stomach. They hadn't talked, she realized. Not about their
feelings for each other. Not about their expectations. Not
about anything. Other than a murmur or a sigh, a whisper
of pleasure, neither of them had really spoken to the
other. In truth, after they'd shared that first kiss out in
the storm, nothing had been said at all.

Panic had her heart racing. Desiree turned her head to
look at Alex. He was awake, his eyes trained on her. An
hour ago those eyes had been warm and smoky with desire. Now they were cool and clear. He certainly didn't
resemble a man who'd just discovered he was in love
with her. She swallowed past the nerves tightening her
throat. "Regrets?" she asked him.

"No. No regrets."

Well, at least that was good news.

"What about you? Are you sorry about what happened
between us?"

"No. Not at all," she told him, feeling the noose of
tense nerves loosen a fraction. "I've never made love in
a rainstorm before. Or in a gazebo for that matter."

Alex scrubbed a hand over his face and sighed. "Do you want me to apologize?"

"Apologize?" she asked, confused. "Whatever for?"

"For...for coming at you like I did. Hell, I practically attacked you out there." He sat up in the bed, shoved his hands through his hair. "I've never done anything like that before. It was crazy. I don't know what got into me. One minute I was going after you to tell you Maggie was here and the next thing I knew, I was kissing you."

"Don't you dare apologize to me, Alexander Stone. It was wonderful. *You* were wonderful." Feeling alive and happy, she snuggled over to him, ran her fingers along the side of his jaw. "Next time, maybe we could try the lake. I've always wondered what it would be like to make love in a river or a lake."

He went still. The hand stroking her back froze midway down her spine. "I'm not sure that's such a good idea."

Her stomach pitched. She swallowed back the panic rising like bile in her throat. "Which one isn't a good idea? The next time? Or the lake?"

"Both."

Her heart slammed against her ribs painfully, but this time instead of running to lick her wounds, she forced herself to concentrate on the way he had looked at her, the way he had loved her. She was going to fight for that love. Even if that meant fighting him. "Listen to me, Alexander Stone. I love you. You got that? I love you. Now. Always."

"You c—"

"I love you," she shouted, fear clawing at her chest. "I suggest you get used to hearing it because that's not going to change." She didn't know how to convince this man, who was so afraid of believing in forevers, that love didn't come with a warranty. All she could do was promise to give him all the love in her heart, and hope it would be enough.

"I love you," she repeated softly. "And someday, maybe if I tell you often enough, you'll start to believe me. And then maybe, just maybe, you'll even be brave enough to admit you feel the same way about me."

The woman was trouble. He'd known it the first time he'd set eyes on her, Alex told himself the next morning. Keeping an ear tuned for Kevin's arrival, he paced the length of the cabin, but his thoughts returned to Desiree. You'd think a man with his supposed intelligence would have the sense not to mess around with a stick of dynamite packing a lit fuse. Obviously he didn't. Because he'd allowed her to explode into his life and rip a hole the size of the Mississippi River right through his heart.

He was in love with her.

"Oh, Lord," Alex muttered. Feeling as though the wind had been knocked out of him, he sank to the couch. He was in love with Desiree.

Hell, he hadn't had a prayer—not from the moment she'd wrapped her arms around him and kissed him for stopping her wedding—or at least for stopping what he had thought was her wedding.

He buried his head in his hands. He should have realized how deeply he'd started to fall when he'd begun to think that her naming her pets after characters from Tennessee Williams's plays was charming instead of strange.

Alex groaned. Man, he was in trouble. Chin-deep, sinking-fast trouble. Despite all of his promises to himself, all the examples he'd had that proved what a dangerous thing love was, he'd gone and fallen in love with her, anyway. And he didn't have a clue as to what he was going to do about it.

A part of him wanted to believe that she loved him. But he knew what a fickle thing love was and just how quickly it could be snatched away. As much as she claimed to love him now, however much she might actually love him now, that didn't mean it was going to last. He knew, probably better than she did, just how unlikely that scenario was. Sweat broke out across his brow as he recalled his parents' soul-shattering anguish each time love had soured for them.

He remembered all too easily that sickening sense of loss and the middle-of-the-night panic that had plagued him with each divorce, each relationship that ended. Because each divorce for his parents had meant a divorce for him, too. Each time they lost out on love, so did he.

That misery would be a picnic compared to how he would feel were he to love Desiree, allow himself to believe that she loved him and then lose her. The tap at the door saved him from that despairing thought.

"Hi, bro," Kevin told him when he opened the door. His brother gave him a man hug that was half embrace, half slap on the back. "Thanks for coming to see me in the play."

"We both know that's not the only reason I came, Kev," Alex told him as his brother entered the cottage. While he'd come to discuss law school and his future with Kevin, Alex realized now that his brother had only been a part of the reason. The main reason he'd come back was Desiree.

"If you're going to tell me what an idiot I was for wanting to get married, don't bother. I already know that."

Alex paused and studied his brother. "You don't look too broken up about it." In truth, he'd expected Kevin to be miserable. Their father had always gone into a tailspin of depression following any breakup—be it marriage or romance. But Kevin didn't look depressed. In fact, he looked downright happy.

"I'm not. The truth is, I'm sort of interested in someone else. She's someone I've only discovered recently."

Which just went to prove how reliable love was, Alex thought. "Kevin—"

"Don't worry, Alex. I know what I'm doing. I also know what I want to do with my life." Kevin sat down across from him and looked him square in the eye. In that moment Alex detected a determination, a steel in Kevin that he hadn't seen before. "Now here's what I'd like to do...."

Two hours later Alex stared at his younger brother and wondered how the boy had become a man without him realizing it. "I'm impressed, Kev. You really have thought this thing through."

"You were the one who taught me to sit down and weigh the pros and cons of a situation before making a decision. That's what I did. I know there are still some risks here, the biggest being whether I can convince the world that I'm an actor—one who's worth paying money to see. But you also taught me some rewards were worth the risks."

Had he taught Kevin that? If he had, he'd somehow forgotten that lesson himself. Loving Desiree and believing she would continue to love him was a risk. Surely it was a risk worth taking.

"Come on, Alex. Don't look so grim. You did a good job of raising me. Now it's time for me to take it from here." Kevin gave him a punch to the shoulder. "Remember that time I wanted to make the baseball team in grade school, but was a lousy batter?"

"Yes, I remember."

"You told me that I could do it. You practiced with me every day until I was good enough and made the

team. And when I screwed up and struck out and wanted
to quit, do you remember what you told me?''

Alex thought back to those days so long ago. ''I told
you if you gave up, then being on the team hadn't really
mattered as much to you as you'd thought. If it had, you
would learn from your mistakes and try again. Because
if you want something badly enough, you find a way to
make it happen.''

''I know I'm going to make some mistakes, and I hope
I can learn from them. I want to be an actor. And I'm
going to find a way to make that happen.''

When he shut the door behind his brother a short time
later, Alex wondered if he could learn from the mistakes
he'd seen his parents make. Could he build a life with
Desiree? He wasn't sure he could, but he knew he wanted
to try. The question was would she still give him that
chance? There was only one way to find out, he decided.
Telling himself he might as well go for broke, Alex
picked up the phone and punched out the number to his
office. ''Ms. Crawford, this is Alex Stone. I need you to
get Adam Kennedy at the bank on the phone for me.''

His heart pounding like a drum, Alex swallowed when
the connection was made. Then he dove in and went for
broke. ''Adam. Alex Stone here. I need you to do me a
favor. Do you have any connections with a good jeweler
in the New Orleans area?''

Later that afternoon, Alex opened the velvet-lined box
for what must have been the tenth time in as many
minutes. He stared at the marquis-shaped diamond set in
a thin gold band. Closing the lid, he slipped the box back
into the pocket of his jacket and glanced at his watch
again. It was still too early to spring the offer of dinner
on her. He'd known she was rehearsing all afternoon and
probably hadn't even had time to change yet. Why was
it that time insisted on ticking by so slowly today?

Because he was anxious to see Desiree, to tell her he loved her and ask her to share her life with him. Acid churned in his gut once more as he considered what her answer would be. Moving to the bar, he poured himself a glass of Chardonnay. He'd negotiated ten-million-dollar deals with far less anxiety. He took a taste of the wine. But none of those deals involved his heart.

He put down the glass, unable to even enjoy the fine California vintage for the tension running through him. Restless, he took another look at his watch. Not five minutes had passed since he'd last checked the time, but Alex didn't think he could wait any longer.

Maybe she had cut rehearsal short, he reasoned. She might have even showered by now and could be making dinner plans at this moment. He couldn't wait a moment longer. He didn't think his nerves could take it. Opening the door, he opted to walk down the path that led from his cottage to Magnolia House instead of taking the car.

Anxious, he practically ran the entire distance to Magnolia House. As he entered the house and started down the hall toward Desiree's office, he registered the vases filled with fresh flowers, the polished floors, the gleaming crystal, the sound of china and silver clinking from the ballroom where tables were being readied for tomorrow's grand opening. He registered everything, but his thoughts were focused on the green-eyed woman he'd come to see.

Just before he reached her office, a fresh bout of nerves hit him. An icy chill skipped down his spine. What if this was a mistake? What if her love proved as temporary as that of most people in his life? Swallowing back the apprehension, he patted the pocket that held the diamond ring. He loved Desiree and she'd said she loved him, he told himself. He wanted to marry her—enough to make it happen. Holding on to that thought, he started for her office.

The door was already ajar. As he stepped inside, Alex's gaze swept the office, but found it empty. *She's probably still in the shower after all*, he thought with a smile and headed for the bedroom that adjoined her office.

The smile on his face froze. His heart seemed to stop beating as he stared in the open doorway at Desiree, dressed in a slinky green robe, wrapped in Kevin's arms.

"Oh gosh, Des. I love you," Kevin said. Catching her by the waist, he spun around in a circle with her in his arms.

She tipped back her head in laughter. "I love you, too, you idiot. Now put me down."

Pain ripped through him like a sniper's bullet. So much for her loving him forever. They hadn't even made it to the altar. He'd been a fool to think with Desiree things would be any different.

"Kevin, put me down," Desiree commanded, smacking him on the shoulder.

"Not until you say you'll marry me."

Jealousy clawed at Alex like an angry beast, slicing through the waves of pain. "I suggest you take him up on his proposal, because if you were hoping to get one from me, you're out of luck."

Ten

Desiree jerked her head toward Alex. She sucked in her breath as she stared into his cold, furious eyes. She hadn't thought that a heart could truly break, but now she suspected she'd been wrong. Because right now her heart felt as though it were breaking into a million pieces.

"Of course, you'll still have to wait until Kevin's of age to have access to his trust fund," Alex told her, his voice as cold as an Arctic wind and every bit as chilling.

Releasing her from his embrace, Kevin gave her a puzzled look, then swung his gaze to his brother. "How the devil did my trust fund get into this?"

"I'll let Desiree explain that to you, little brother. But if I were you, I'd think twice about marrying her."

"Marrying… Now, wait a minute," Kevin shot back. "I don't know what it is you think you saw just now, but—"

"I think it's pretty obvious what I saw. The woman

who last night claimed to love me, who said she would always love me, in the arms of my brother telling him she loved him.''

Desiree flinched at the condemnation in Alex's eyes as he looked at her. He thought she'd betrayed him. She'd known she had a tough road ahead of her. Alex was a man who feared love and was a master of keeping people at arm's length. For him being loved had always been temporary, something that would disappear from his life as the people who'd claimed to love him left him and moved on. Convincing a man who didn't believe in forevers to take a chance that her love for him would be constant wouldn't be easy. She'd known all those things going in, but last night she could have sworn she'd made progress. Even though he hadn't given her the words, she'd been so sure he felt the same way she did. Evidently she'd been wrong. If he had loved her, he could never believe she would go from his arms to his brother's. And the fool man didn't even consider that there could be an explanation. He'd automatically decided she was guilty.

"Are you nuts? What you saw just now was—"

"No." Desiree placed a hand on Kevin's arm to silence him as her own anger began to buffer some of the pain. "I don't think your brother is interested in any explanations from either of us. He's already made up his mind."

"Yeah, but—"

"Am I right, Alex? Explanations aren't really necessary, are they? Because you've already condemned me."

"You're good, Desiree. I'll give you that. You play the indignant innocent very well. But then you're an actress and I guess you've had lots of practice."

He didn't know just how good an actress she was, Desiree thought silently, stinging from the bite of his words. She could feel Kevin simmering with anger beside her, but Kevin wasn't really at issue here. What lay between her and Alex went far deeper than a simple misunderstanding or jealousy. At the heart of it was his lack of faith and trust in her. Capturing Kevin's hand, she squeezed it hard and pleaded with her eyes for him to say nothing more. She saw his reluctance and was grateful at his silence. Turning back to face Alex, she asked, "Was there anything else you wanted, Alex? We have a show to get ready for."

His face was dark with anger as he lifted his gaze from their joined hands. Desiree had to force herself not to step back at the raw fury in his eyes. "If you marry her, Kevin, it'll be the biggest mistake of your life."

She hadn't thought it possible for him to hurt her any more than he already had. But his words slashed through her like a knife.

"You're a damn fool," Kevin shouted, breaking free of her grip on his hands.

"Kevin, please. Don't—"

"It's all right, Desiree. Kevin's right. I am a fool. Fool enough to allow myself to fall in love with you."

Desiree's heart seemed to sputter and stop before it began to work again. How many times had she prayed to hear him say those words to her, longed to hear him tell her. But not like this. Not when he was angry and in pain.

"I was even fool enough to believe we could have one of those fairy-tale endings of yours." All of the anger seemed to leave him at once. In its place was only a deep sadness. "But then I never did believe in fairy tales. So maybe you made the right choice after all. Things would never have worked between us."

He shifted his attention to his brother. "Forget everything I said, Kevin. Go ahead and marry her. I hope the two of you will be happy.''

Desiree felt as though he'd slapped her. He was giving up on her, she realized as he turned and started to leave. She didn't mean enough to him for him to even try to work things out. Instead, he'd chosen to walk away from what they had together rather than to take a chance on their love.

Kevin looked at her. "Des?"

She knew he was waiting for her to say something, to stop Alex from walking out the door. She shook her head. If she meant so little to him, then there was no point in fighting any longer.

"Alex, wait," Kevin called out as his brother turned and started to leave.

When Alex paused, Kevin shot her another look, but she shook her head again. He made an exasperated sound. "What about the show tomorrow night? Are you going to come?"

"Under the circumstances, I don't think that would be such a good idea. But good luck. To both of you." Then he turned and started to leave.

"Wait!"

When Alex stopped and looked at him again, Kevin said, "You promised me you'd come to the show. You agreed to see me on stage."

"I'm sure I'll get to see you perform another time. Right now, I'd just like to get my things and go back to Boston. I'm sorry, but you'll just have to understand."

"I don't understand," Kevin argued. "You taught me that I needed to be a man of my word. I always thought you were one. You gave me your word you'd come see me in the play tomorrow night, and I'm holding you to it."

"All right," Alex said, his jaw clenching. "I'll come

tomorrow night. But as soon as the play's over, I'm going back to Boston.''

Desiree watched Alex walk out of her office and close the door. The minute he was gone she turned on Kevin. ''Why did you do that? You know he didn't want to come.''

''One of us had to do something to stop him from leaving. And since you obviously weren't going to even try to explain things, I decided it was up to me. Holding him to his promise to come to the play was all I could come up with on such short notice.''

''You should have let him go, Kevin. There's no reason for him to stay.''

''No reason for him to stay!'' Kevin dragged a hand through his hair, a mannerism so similar to Alex's that it caused her another pang. ''I swear, I don't know who's the bigger idiot, Des. You or my brother.''

''Gee thanks.''

He grabbed her by the shoulders. ''Didn't you hear what he said? Alex told you he loved you! But the idiot thinks you and I are involved. You need to explain to him he was wrong about us.''

She shook her head. ''I'm not going to explain anything to him, and I don't want you to explain it, either. Alex made up his mind. He didn't want any explanations. He wanted an out and he found one. Telling him he made a mistake about us isn't going to change the fact that he wanted to walk away. And now he has.''

Kevin slapped his hand to his forehead and lifted his eyes heavenward. ''Dear Lord, when I fall in love again, please don't let me become dumb and blind like these two.'' When he finished his prayer, he looked at her again. ''Listen to me, Desiree Mason. The man just said that he loves you. As far as I know Alex has never told *any* woman he's loved her before.''

"If he'd *really* loved me, he could never have believed I'd betray him," she snapped. "Alex wants guarantees. Well, love doesn't come with any. It's a gamble. You put your heart on the line and take a chance by trusting the other person. Without trust, you don't stand a chance."

Kevin gripped her hands and looked down at her out of serious brown eyes. "Listen to me. I know my brother. If he says he loves you, you can bet that he means it. Love is not a word he takes lightly. That's why it was always so hard on him when our folks jumped on and off that matrimonial merry-go-round."

"I know all about his insecurities and what your parents' divorces and marriages have done to him. Why do you think I tried so hard?"

"Try again. If you love him, forgive him and give him a second chance."

Beneath the anger and hurt, she did still love him, Desiree admitted. "I don't know, Kevin. I— What's that?" She frowned at the sound of raised voices coming from down the hall.

"Now which one of these doors did you say goes to my little girl's office?"

"Daddy?" Desiree whispered, surprised to hear her father's voice.

"Your father's Cary Grant?" Kevin asked.

Desiree smiled. "No, but you're close. He's got a part as an extra on a remake of *To Catch a Thief* that's starting next month." And according to her mother, her father had been studying the original movie for weeks.

"And?" Kevin prompted, obviously needing more of an explanation.

"And Daddy likes to be prepared in case he's ever asked to step in for the lead. So, he's been studying the original version which starred—"

"Cary Grant," Kevin finished.

"Yes. So you're probably about to meet Henry Mason's rendition of Cary Grant." She laughed at Kevin's baffled expression. "Be grateful, when my sister Lorelei got married a few months ago, she had Spencer Tracy giving her away."

"Cool."

Her folks were pretty cool, Desiree thought, as the door burst open and in walked her father with Alex. "Here you go, young man." Her father slipped Alex a bill. "You can just leave the bags by the reception desk."

"I…uh…thank you," Alex replied.

Desiree didn't know which was more amusing—her father's attempt at a British accent or the look on Alex's face at being mistaken for a bellman.

As though Alex had sensed her thoughts, he shifted his gaze to meet hers. But then her father came forward and swept her up into his arms. "Daddy, you came!"

"Of course I came. Did you think for a minute I'd miss my little girl's opening night?"

"But how?" She looked at the face of the man who'd always believed in her and her dreams, the man who, like her, believed in fairy tales. There were lines on that face now, and the hair that had once been dark brown was a distinguished silver. The eyes that were once a vivid blue were a bit faded now, but they still held that spark of life and love. She hugged him again. "I'm so glad you came. But tell me what happened. Mom said you couldn't get away because of the movie."

Her father puffed up his chest. "I simply told J.B.— he's the director," he explained feigning a British accent. "I said, J.B. old chap, I have to get some time off to see my little girl on her opening night or I'll bloody well quit."

"Poppycock," her mother said from the doorway.

''The star of the film took the weekend off, and production shut down. So the rest of the cast got the weekend off, too.''

''Well, I *would have* told J.B. I had to have time off if he hadn't said we were free.''

Her mother shot her father a reproving look before holding her arms open for Desiree. She hugged her close, then held her at arm's length. ''How are you, darling?''

''Great. Just fine.''

Her mother gave her a searching look, then shifted her gaze to Kevin. ''Is this the young man I've been hearing about? The one you've been talking to your sister about, but haven't bothered to even mention to me?''

''I certainly hope so, Mrs. Mason,'' Kevin said with a grin. Stepping forward he took her mother's hand and kissed it. But I suspect it was my brother you've been hearing about. I'm Kevin Stone, a friend of your daughter's.''

Desiree nearly groaned. She cut a glance to the doorway, but thankfully Alex was gone. She was going to kill Clea, she promised—right after she murdered Kevin. She glared at Kevin, but his eyes were on her mother. Not that she blamed him. Even though she was past fifty, her mother was still a beautiful woman. With her red hair, green eyes and trim figure, she still reminded Desiree of Maureen O'Hara.

''Please call me Abby,'' her mother replied with an answering smile. ''And tell me, Kevin, is this brother of yours as handsome and charming as you?''

Kevin laughed. ''Some people might say so, but personally, I think I'm the one who got the looks and charm in the family. But Alex is a nice guy all the same. You just met him as a matter of fact. He was the guy who carried in your bags.''

''The bellman?''

"He's not a bellman. He's a lawyer."

Her mother frowned as she digested that news. "Evidently, the legal profession isn't as profitable as it once was if he's moonlighting as a bellman."

"Wow, cousin Des," her cousin Lilah exclaimed from the doorway. "If all the men in this town are as good-looking as that bellman that just brought my bag inside, I just might have to move down south myself."

"He's a lawyer," her mother explained. "It seems lawyers aren't making as much money as they used to. At least not here."

Desiree sighed and snagged a gaping Kevin by the elbow. "Come on, Kevin. Let me introduce you to my father. And you remember my cousin Lilah? She stopped by to visit last week."

"Oh, yes. The actress," Kevin replied.

By the time introductions were made, a tour was given and her parents and cousin were settled for the night, Desiree was running on empty. Her anger at Alex had long since faded, and she had hoped all evening that he would come by so the two of them could talk. But he hadn't.

Restless, Desiree slipped on her sandals and let herself outside. Tonight there was no storm, no flashes of lightning, no rumbles of thunder. No Alex appearing out of the darkness like some Viking warrior to take her in his arms and make love to her.

The sky was clear, with a lovers' moon and thousands of stars sparkling against a canvas of black. As she walked along the path, the scent of night jasmine drifted on a breeze. Hugging her arms to herself, she continued to walk and allowed her mind to drift. She thought of the dozens of details that needed to be handled tomorrow before the theater's opening. She thought about her parents' surprise visit and the second unexpected visit by her cousin Lilah. Desiree grinned as she recalled the look on Kevin's face when he'd seen her pretty blond cousin again. Something told her Kevin's little romantic setback wouldn't be bothering him much longer.

Too bad the same couldn't be said for her, she decided, as her thoughts turned to Alex. The foolish man had been way out of line, she told herself. If he'd loved her as he'd claimed, he would have trusted her. But then, she'd been too angry and hurt at the time to even offer him an explanation. Maybe Kevin was right. Maybe he did deserve another chance after all.

Who was she kidding? She loved Alex and she wasn't ready to give up on him and her dreams for them yet. Picking up her pace, Desiree broke into a run and raced down the path. As she came around the bend she stopped. Disappointment hit her like a blow to the chest and she pressed her hand against her heart. The cottage was in darkness. No car sat parked in the driveway. Alex was gone.

"Man of his word, my eye," Alex muttered as he dressed for the dinner theater opening the next evening. His brother had missed his calling as an attorney, Alex fumed as he fastened the cuff links on his shirt. The kid was a master manipulator. He'd known exactly which buttons to push to get him to agree to come back tonight for the play.

He slipped the tie around his neck and stared at his reflection in the mirror. He looked like hell, Alex decided—which was exactly the way he felt. Giving up on the tie, he placed both hands on the dresser and leaned forward. He closed his eyes. Not even spending the night in a hotel room in the city away from Desiree, away from this place had helped. He hadn't slept a wink for thinking about her—remembering what it had been like to hold her in his arms, to make love to her, to hear her say she loved him.

Nor had it eased the torment and betrayal he'd felt at discovering her with Kevin. Opening his eyes, Alex looked once more into the mirror, but this time instead of his own reflection, it was that crushed expression on Desiree's face that stared back at him. Instead of finding guilt or even shame in those big green eyes of hers, there had been hurt. Hurt and disappointment. She's an actress, he reminded himself as he tried to banish the images of her from his thoughts. He fumbled with the tie again. But her pain had seemed real. So had her anger.

Straightening the tie, he paused. What if he'd been wrong? But if she'd been innocent, why hadn't she denied his accusations? Why hadn't Kevin?

Because he hadn't been wrong, Alex told himself. He'd seen them together, heard Kevin propose to her. And Desiree had told Kevin she loved him. Pain ripped through him again, twisting in his gut like a knife.

Retrieving his jacket, Alex slipped it on and glanced at his watch. There was enough time to finish packing before heading over to Magnolia House, he decided. As soon as the play was over and he'd told Kevin goodbye, he could leave. No point in hanging around until morning, he told himself as he loaded his shirts into the suitcase. Even if he sat in the airport all night, it would be better than spending another night here with memories of Desiree everywhere he turned.

He grabbed his shaving gear and began to stuff it into his bag when he caught sight of a familiar bundle of black fur in the doorway.

"What are you doing here?"

Maggie meowed in answer before strolling into the room as though she had every right to be there. That was the problem. She belonged with Desiree and maybe even

Kevin did, too, but he didn't. Reaching into his bag, Alex grabbed the vial of antihistamine tablets and shook one out into his palm. He tossed it back and chased it down with a sip of water, ignoring the Chardonnay he'd poured earlier but hadn't bothered to drink.

"At least once I'm out of here, I won't have to worry about my allergies kicking up because you barged in on me. I bet Desiree doesn't even know you're here, does she?"

Maggie gave him another meow and proceeded to rub against his pant leg. "Great. Just what I need—a mess of black fur on my tux pants," he told her, but made no attempt to shoo her away. Instead, he stuffed his socks and handkerchiefs into the suitcase pockets, taking care not to step on the cat as she moved back and forth against him.

"I'm leaving tonight, so you're going to have to find yourself another rubbing post," he told her as he continued to pack his things.

Maggie weaved her little body in and out of his legs, meowing what sounded like protests. Alex chuckled at the absurd notion and reached for the wineglass. "Does that mean you're going to miss me?" he asked, and felt a strange little pang at the thought of not seeing the cat again.

That thought brought him up short. Setting down the glass, Alex scrubbed a hand over his face. "Just goes to show you how crazy I've become since meeting the woman. Now I'm even talking to a cat."

But when Maggie pushed up on her hind legs to nudge her head in his hand for a pet, Alex gave up on packing. "All right. I admit it. I'm going to miss you, too," he told her. He stooped down to scratch Maggie behind her ears and spied a length of white ribbon on the floor peeking out from beneath the bed—the ribbon that had been on Desiree's nightgown the night they'd made love.

Picking up the strip of satin, he ran it across his fingertips. As he did so, he caught Desiree's scent and found himself hurled back to that night with her in his arms. Still clutching the piece of satin, he sank to the bed and buried his head in his hands. Suddenly he thought about his life before Desiree. All the years without those emotional highs and lows that he'd seen his parents struggle with. He'd been content and not unhappy. He'd even had a satisfying sex life.

Then he thought of these past few weeks with Desiree. He'd never felt so alive, so much a participant in life as opposed to an observer. And their lovemaking—it had been like nothing he'd ever known before. No woman had ever made him feel as she did. He had never wanted any woman more. Acid churned in his stomach as he thought about going back to his old life—to a life without Desiree. He didn't want to, he realized. Wasn't even sure if he could. Heaven help him, he thought. He was desperately in love with her, and she was going to marry his brother.

As though sensing his grief, Maggie hopped up onto the bed beside him and proceeded to nuzzle his hand. "Kevin was right," he told Maggie. "I am an idiot. A first-rate fool. I fell in love with her. Me, Alex Stone. I always swore I'd never be like my father. I'd never let myself be ruled by my emotions. But I did, and I was foolish enough to let myself believe that she could love me." He laughed at his own stupidity.

"I was even crazy enough to think we might have a future together," he told the silent Maggie. "I guess I was hoping for one of those fairy-tale endings she's so big on. How could I have been so stupid? What kind of man lets himself believe in fairy-tales, anyway?"

"Maybe a man who's in love," Kevin answered from the doorway.

Alex jerked his head up to look at his brother. "How long have you been standing there?"

"Long enough to know that you really are in love with Desiree." Kevin came into the room. "I wasn't so sure when you disappeared yesterday. But judging from what I just heard and seeing that cat on your lap, yeah, I'd have to say you've got it pretty bad."

Putting Maggie aside, Alex stood and dusted off his pants. "I'll get over it," Alex assured him. He shut the lid of the suitcase and snapped the locks. After putting the bag on the floor, he turned to face his brother.

"Suit yourself," Kevin told him. "But I can't see why."

Alex stared at Kevin and wondered which of them was the craziest. "I'd say the fact that you're in love with her and she's going to marry you would be reason enough."

"You're right about one thing. I do love Desiree— although not in the way you think. In fact, in case you've forgotten, just a few weeks ago I was ready to marry someone else."

"I haven't forgotten," Alex shot back. And it had bothered him how quickly Kevin had bounced back. "But as you pointed out to me recently, you're a grown man. I would hope you wouldn't be foolish enough to ask Desiree to marry you because you're on the rebound."

"No. I wouldn't be that foolish," Kevin assured him. "Make no mistake about it. I do love Desiree. I have for a long time. In fact, I've been asking Desiree to marry me at least twice a week since the first day I met her. She's a beautiful, fascinating woman and I adore her."

The glimmer of hope that had flickered inside him died

a swift death. "Then, I guess you're very happy that she's agreed to marry you."

"That's where there seems to be a misunderstanding. You see, as far as I know, Desiree and I aren't getting married."

Alex narrowed his eyes. "What do you mean, you aren't getting married. I heard the two of you. You told her you loved her, proposed to her, and she told you she loved you."

"You know, big brother. For a guy with a genius IQ, sometimes you really can be pretty dumb. What you heard was two friends joking around. Desiree and I do love each other—but not in that way. The lady doesn't want me and she's not going to marry me. The foolish female actually prefers you."

Alex stared at his brother, at the grin spreading across his face, the laughter in his eyes. "But you asked her to marry you."

"I told you. It's a standard joke between us."

"But you said you were interested in somebody else," Alex reminded him as he digested what Kevin had told him.

"I am. But that person isn't Desiree. It's her cousin Lilah. I met her when she visited Desiree last week. I spoke to her on the phone a few days ago and saw her again yesterday. You'll meet her tonight at the opening. You're sitting with Desiree's family."

Alex sat down on the bed. His head whirled with what Kevin had told him. "Then you and Desiree aren't getting married? She's not really in love with you?"

"Nope."

"Why didn't she tell me? Why didn't you?"

"It looked to me like you'd already made up your mind and condemned her. She'd have taken my head off if I'd said anything after she'd told me not to."

Alex shoved a hand through his hair. "Yeah. I guess I did jump the gun." What he hadn't done was trust in her love for him, Alex admitted silently. He'd decided without giving her any chance to explain that her love had proved as temporary as he'd always believed it would.

Kevin leaned against the dresser and grinned. "It was quite an interesting sight to see my heretofore unflappable brother lose his cool over a woman."

"Don't remind me."

"Did you mean what you said earlier? Do you really love her?" Kevin asked.

"Yes. I love her."

"The words are easy. It's the rest of it that's hard. Desiree said you're big on guarantees, but that love doesn't come with any. I guess she's right."

"I guess she is," Alex admitted.

"I know it used to tear you up every time Dad or your mother went through another divorce, Alex. I always figured that was the reason you never really let anyone get close to you except for me. But Desiree's not the kind of woman who would settle for being kept at arm's length emotionally. It's either all or nothing with her."

"I know that," Alex told him.

"Yeah, but do you love her enough? Enough to trust her and her feelings for you? Enough to risk being hurt by her if things don't work out?"

Alex stared at the young man who had been more son than brother to him and then down at the ribbon in his hand. He thought of his life before Desiree, the life that stretched out before him without her. He had been only half-alive before meeting her. He didn't want to go back to that life again. "Yes," Alex told him. "I love her and I want her—enough to do whatever I have to do to get her back."

Kevin smiled. "Glad to hear it. But I'm not the one you're going to have to convince, you know. Desiree is. She was pretty steamed at you yesterday. In fact, as far as I could tell, she was still steamed at you when I saw her a little while ago."

"Can't say that I blame her." And he didn't. He'd been way out of line. "Maybe I should go talk to her," Alex offered and was halfway to the door when Kevin stopped him.

"I don't think that's such a good idea. At least not right now. She's all worked up about the show, and to be honest, just the mention of your name sets off her temper. When I told her that I'd reserved you a seat at the table with her family for the show, she told me she didn't care where I put you just so long as she didn't have to speak to you again. Then she slammed the door closed in my face. I think you've got yourself a pretty deep hole to dig out of, big brother."

"Don't you think I know that?" Exasperated, he dragged a hand through his hair. "How am I supposed to dig myself out of that hole if she won't even speak to me?"

"You know, it's kind of nice to be the one to dispense brotherly advice for a change," Kevin told him, that infernal grin spreading across his face again.

"I hope you're enjoying yourself."

"I certainly am."

"In the meantime, my life's going to hell."

"Don't worry, big brother, I've got a plan...."

Eleven

The blasted man hadn't come—not even for Kevin's sake. Desiree slipped her feet into the white satin pumps and reached for the wedding veil. Each time her gaze had strayed from the stage, she'd told herself she'd only been scoping out the audience, checking on her family. But unerringly she continued to zero in on that one empty seat at the table with her family where Alex was supposed to be.

As was always the case, now that she'd had time to get over her initial anger, the real hurt had set in. She still loved him. Despite everything that had happened, his outrageous accusations, his obvious distrust of her and his own reluctance to admit he loved her, nothing had changed the simple fact that she loved Alex. And deep in her heart, she admitted, she had been hanging on to the fact that he had said he loved her. Idiot that she was, she'd actually thought he would come tonight and try to set things right between them. Obviously he didn't love her enough.

"There you go," Mindy told her as she did up the last of the buttons at the back of the wedding gown. She sighed. "You make such a beautiful bride, Desiree. It's a shame that you're only getting married in the play and not for real."

Desiree began securing the veil of lace to her hair with pins. Fool that she was she'd had thoughts along those same lines herself just a few days ago—even a few hours ago. She glanced from her reflection in the mirror to the woman standing behind her dressed in an emerald bridesmaid's dress. "Thanks. But I think getting married in the play is about all the excitement I can handle at the moment."

"I guess you're right. But, you know, some of us in the cast had sort of thought that maybe something would sort of develop between you and Alex Stone." The other woman began to smooth out the skirt of the wedding gown. "I mean neither one of you is involved with anyone else, and whenever the two of you were in the same room together, it was like... *Zap!* There was a spark between the two of you that seemed strong enough to cause a power outage."

"Well, looks like that spark turned out to be nothing more than a fizzle," Desiree said, with a lightness of tone she was far from feeling.

"A pity, too. He was one sexy-looking guy. The two of you would've made a great-looking bride and groom." She paused. "Listen, Desiree, if you and he—"

Snagging the bridal bouquet from her dressing table, Desiree turned to her friend. "Heavens. We'd better get moving or they're going to start the scene without us."

"They wouldn't dare. After all, you're not only the

star, you're the owner,'' Mindy informed her as she followed her out of the dressing room.

"Well, right now, I'm a very nervous owner. I want Magnolia House to be a big success.''

"Judging from the full tables out there and the audience's applause, you're going to get your wish. You've got a hit on your hands, Des.''

"On *our* hands,'' Desiree corrected. "I just hope you're right and we're a smash. Ready for the last act?''

"You bet,'' Mindy told her as they took their places on the stage with the other members of the cast.

"OK guys, you're all doing great. Now let's knock everyone's socks off with the grand finale.''

The curtain started to rise and Desiree found herself holding her breath as she swept her gaze out over the audience. Mindy had been right. They did have a full house, and judging by the expressions on the faces of Magnolia House's opening night customers, her dinner theater was on its way to being a success. Cutting a glance to her family's table, she winked at her father and had to bite back another pang of disappointment. Alex's chair remained empty. He hadn't come.

"Dearly beloved. We are gathered here today...''

Forcing herself to concentrate on the role she was playing, Desiree tried to lose herself in the character. She was a woman on the verge of marrying the wrong man—the brother of the only man she'd ever loved—a man whose stubborn pride had forced them apart.

But unlike her character, her own life wouldn't reflect the happy ending of her play. Not without Alex. Pushing aside that gloomy thought, Desiree listened to Charlie deliver his lines and tried not to think of that day six weeks ago when Alex had burst into the room to interrupt the rehearsal.

"If there should be anyone present who can give just

cause why this man and this woman should not be joined in holy wedlock," Charlie continued with all the pomp and authority of the clergyman he pretended to be. "Let him speak now or forever hold his peace."

"Stop!"

Desiree felt her heart sputter at the sound of that voice. It was her ears playing tricks on her, she told herself. It was Kevin. He had only *sounded* like Alex just now because the two of them were brothers and her head had been filled with thoughts of Alex.

"I demand you stop this wedding at once!"

She wasn't imagining things. It *was* Alex's voice. Hands trembling, she gripped the stem of her bouquet and whipped around to stare at the tall, raven-haired man with a warrior's eyes racing down the aisle of the theater to the stage. Her pulse kicked in at triple speed as she watched him climb up the stairs to the stage and march over to her. Her heart bursting with hope and love, she called on every ounce of her training not to break into a smile.

"Des," her groom prompted.

"How dare you?" she demanded, trying to sound outraged as her role dictated when, in truth, she was overcome with joy. He had come. Alex had come after all.

"Quite easily," Alex delivered the line convincingly, never once taking his eyes off her face.

Was that nervousness she read in his eyes? Alex Stone nervous? Even if the stage were unfamiliar territory, the man never seemed the least bit intimidated by anything. It hardly seemed possible that he was nervous or uncomfortable now—especially considering he'd delivered his lines like a pro, while she...she was not only having a difficult time remembering her lines, but had already missed one cue.

"There's no way I'm going to allow you to marry my brother," he told her.

The round of gasps went up from the bridal party, and Desiree did her best to glare furiously as the role demanded. She suspected she failed miserably.

"Stay out of this," O'Reilly, playing the part of her groom, demanded. He stepped forward and met Alex toe-to-toe just as he'd rehearsed the scene with Kevin. "I'm of age and I don't need your consent to get married. I can marry Kate or anyone I choose to."

"That might be true, and you're welcome to marry anyone else you want to. But you aren't going to marry Desiree because I'm not going to let her marry you."

Desiree caught the pained looked on her groom's face. Evidently Alex wasn't as caught up in his role as she'd thought. Not if he called her "Desiree" instead of "Kate" as the script specified.

"And just what gives you the right to say who I can or can't marry?"

"The right of the man who loves you."

She caught the pleading look in O'Reilly's eyes, telling her that Alex was screwing up big-time—at least as far as the script went. Desiree ignored her costar. No way did she care about the play at the moment. Her eyes remained locked on Alex.

He *was* nervous, she realized, if the way his Adam's apple was bobbing beneath his loosened tie was any indication. And that darned tie of his, it looked like it had been through a wringer. In the time she'd known him, Alex had never seemed anything but impeccably attired. Even during that rainstorm sans tie and with his open shirt, he'd managed an air of complete ease. His Adam's apple bobbed again and deep-sixed what was left of her caution.

"The right of a man who adores you and promises to love you and cherish you."

Charlie made a strangled sound behind her. O'Reilly, the groom, scrubbed a hand down his face. The heck with the play, Desiree thought. Alex and their future was more important. "All of that sounds great, but loving someone takes a lot more than just being able to say the words."

"I know—"

"For me it means marriage."

He fumbled in his pants' pocket. "I know—"

"And trust, believing in the other person no matter what happens."

"I know that too and I—"

"But mostly it means taking a chance on finding that happy ending just like in the fairy tales." She held her breath and waited, prayed he did love her enough.

"I never believed in marriage or fairy tales. Never wanted to believe in either of them," Alex told her, his voice just a shade less than belligerent. He took the flowers from her fingers and tossed them to the floor. He shoved a box into her hands. "You made me want to believe in both. That's why I bought you this."

Desiree opened the box. She stared down at the marquis-shaped diamond ring nestled against a bed of black velvet, then looked back up at Alex's face. The nervousness was still there, but there was also that warrior's determination shining in his eyes again.

"I love you. I want to marry you and take a shot at that happy ending."

"Oh, Alex," she said overwhelmed. "I don't know what to say."

He removed the ring from the box she was holding with unsteady fingers, then took her left hand into his. "A simple yes would do for starters. And maybe...maybe you could even manage 'I love you, too.'"

"Yes," she whispered.

"Thank God," he murmured as he slid the ring onto her finger and pulled her into his arms.

Desiree dropped the ring box. "I love you, too," she told him just before his mouth captured hers in a soul-melting kiss. And if she'd had any doubts about Alex's love for her, he'd answered them in that kiss.

"I love you," he whispered, then dipped down for another kiss before she had a chance to say a word. And when he finally released her mouth and lifted her up into his arms, Desiree could have sworn she heard applause and shouts of "Encore." But she was too busy planning that happy ending to bother coming back to take her bow.

*   *   *   *   *

Watch for Metsy Hingle's next sensuous love story,
THE BODYGUARD AND THE BRIDESMAID,
coming May 1998
from Silhouette Desire

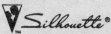

Take 4 bestselling love stories FREE
Plus get a FREE surprise gift!

Special Limited-time Offer

Mail to Sihouette Reader Service™

P.O. Box 609
Fort Erie, Ontario
L2A 5X3

YES! Please send me 4 free Silhouette Desire® novels and my free surprise gift. Then send me 6 brand-new novels every month, which I will receive months before they appear in bookstores. Bill me at the low price of $3.49 each plus 25¢ delivery and GST*. That's the complete price and a savings of over 10% off the cover prices—quite a bargain! I understand that accepting the books and gift places me under no obligation ever to buy any books. I can always return a shipment and cancel at any time. Even if I never buy another book from Silhouette, the 4 free books and the surprise gift are mine to keep forever.

326 SEN CF2S

Name	(PLEASE PRINT)
Address	Apt. No.
City	Province	Postal Code

This offer is limited to one order per household and not valid to present Silhouette Desire® subscribers. *Terms and prices are subject to change without notice. Canadian residents will be charged applicable provincial taxes and GST.

CDES-696   ©1990 Harlequin Enterprises Limited

ALICIA SCOTT

Continues the twelve-book series— 36 Hours—in March 1998 with Book Nine

PARTNERS IN CRIME

The storm was over, and Detective Jack Stryker finally had a prime suspect in Grand Springs' high-profile murder case. But beautiful Josie Reynolds wasn't about to admit to the crime— nor did Jack want her to. He believed in her innocence, and he teamed up with the alluring suspect to prove it. But was he playing it by the book—or merely blinded by love?

For Jack and Josie and *all* the residents of Grand Springs, Colorado, the storm-induced blackout was just the beginning of 36 Hours that changed *everything!* You won't want to miss a single book.

Available at your favorite retail outlet.

SC36HRS9

BESTSELLING AUTHORS
IN THE SPOTLIGHT

WE'RE SHINING THE SPOTLIGHT ON SIX OF OUR STARS!

Harlequin and Silhouette have selected stories from several of their bestselling authors to give you six sensational reads. These star-powered romances are bound to please!

THERE'S A PRICE TO PAY FOR STARDOM... AND IT'S LOW

$1.99 U.S.
$2.50 CAN.
Special Offer

As a special offer, these six outstanding books are available from Harlequin and Silhouette for only $1.99 in the U.S. and $2.50 in Canada. Watch for these titles:

At the Midnight Hour—**Alicia Scott**
Joshua and the Cowgirl—**Sherryl Woods**
Another Whirlwind Courtship—**Barbara Boswell**
Madeleine's Cowboy—**Kristine Rolofson**
Her Sister's Baby—**Janice Kay Johnson**
One and One Makes Three—**Muriel Jensen**

Available in March 1998
at your favorite retail outlet.

PBAIS

Return to the Towers!

In March
New York Times bestselling author

NORA ROBERTS

brings us to the Calhouns' fabulous
Maine coast mansion and reveals the
tragic secrets hidden there for generations.

For all his degrees, Professor Max Quartermain has a
lot to learn about love—and luscious Lilah Calhoun is
just the woman to teach him. Ex-cop Holt Bradford is
as prickly as a thornbush—until Suzanna Calhoun's
special touch makes love blossom in his heart.
And all of them are caught in the race to solve
the generations-old mystery of a priceless
lost necklace…and a timeless love.

Lilah and Suzanna
THE Calhoun Women

**A special 2-in-1 edition containing
FOR THE LOVE OF LILAH and
SUZANNA'S SURRENDER**

Available at your favorite retail outlet.

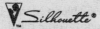